Until Now

DR. MARCIA E. JACKSON

Cocoon to Wings
PUBLISHING

Printed in the United States of America
ISBN: 978-1-7334864-8-4 (Paperback)
ISBN: 978-1-7334864-9-1 (Digital)

Library of Congress Control Number: 2020906052

Published by Cocoon to Wings Publishing
7810 Gall Blvd, #311
Zephyrhills, FL 33541
www.StephanieOutten.com
(813) 906-WING (9464)

Book design by Ereka Thomas Designs.

Until Now

Contents

Foreword

While growing up in Louisiana, I never had much appreciation for the unique and sometimes positive aspects of the state. Then, as soon as I moved two-thousand miles away, it's like I became some sort of a Louisiana patriot. The memories that invade my mind bring an appreciation for life like none other. For, you see, it's those memories that kept some of us afloat during those drowning moments in our lives.

Marcia and I grew up and lived a few houses down from each other. Our parents were close friends. We grew up in a neighborhood called "Stoner Hill." Everybody knew everybody and it was hard to get into trouble without everyone knowing. Our grandmothers, aunts, and uncles grew up together as well. We were a tight knit community.

In 1984 I would be afforded an opportunity that would change the course of my life forever. I left my family and friends and didn't look back. I had no idea that nearly thirty something years later Marcia and I would reunite in a way that only God himself could orchestrate. The book, "Fearless Faith," would bring two long lost souls together and create a bond for a lifetime.

I'd prayed and toiled for months asking God to send me the women that he wanted to use. When I initially reached out to Marcia, she wasn't available. So, I moved on to the next woman in line. As we started the project and neared the editing process, one of the ladies informed me that she would not be able to continue with the project. I was deeply disappointed. I went back to the Father and he sent me back to Marcia. This time she said, "Yes."

The timing was perfect and after weeks of writing and meetings with the editor, we were able to pull it together. Marcia's chapter would move you to activate your faith immediately! God, great God!

Psalms 25:5 says, "Guide me in your truth and teach me, for you are the God who saves me. All day long I put my hope in you." As I was reflecting on the main character of *Until Now*, Taryn Madrid, and her struggles as a young woman and later coming to herself through various experiences, I began to think of how gracious God is in bringing us to the end of ourselves before He delivers us. I sat quietly gazing out the window and I said softly, "The end of yourself is a good place to be."

As a woman whose faith has been tried and tested, I believe Christians are growing weary in these dark days of oppression that we live in. Struggles surround us at every corner, and it is hard to stave off the growing fears of uncertainty. We are told in Scripture that these times would come and test the faithful, but how do we keep standing when the ground is trembling, and darkness is filling the sky?

2 Timothy 1:7 says, "For God has not given us a spirit of fear; but of power, and of love, and of a sound mind." Fear is what the enemy uses to take your focus from the truth. When you understand that your hope in Christ is secure, you can cease striving. There is nothing that is going to destroy a believer who is holding onto the promises that Jesus died to give. Your future is never determined by your circumstance. Trials that

you face are only the wind that brings you closer to God. Every single one of your struggles are used by God to equip you for the battles that come against you.

While Taryn struggled early in her life to understand that people don't always tell the truth, she also understood that that was not a reflection of her, but them. Throughout the Bible, God allowed His people to be taken to the end of their own strength but yet they were conquerors over all that came against them. The three Jewish boys were bound and thrown into the furnace for refusing to bow in worship to Nebuchadnezzar in the book of Daniel, yet it was there that they came face to face with the Son of God who protected them from even the smell of fire and smoke.

Young David ran against the giant, Goliath, in the power of the God in whom he trusted. He never doubted that his God could save him as he killed that heathen Philistine with just a stone. It was God who fought their battles and saved them. You need to understand clearly that when you are in Christ, you are a force to be reckoned with!

Beloved, you must understand that no battle you ever face is hopeless. You don't need to run from your problems; you just need to turn to your God! Never lose faith when you get to the end of your ability for it is at that point that you discover the power of God. Jesus paid the price for our redemption and to give us a future with hope. The enemy may prowl around trying to rob you of your joy, but he can never steal the future that Christ paid with his blood.

We are living in a time like no other. We are watching as wars, famines, floods, severe weather, poverty, sickness of all kinds of evil are permeating this entire world. The hearts of many have grown cold as marriages are failing, evil and violence are increasing, and all forms of perversions are becoming common. The only hope we have is the enduring love of Christ who will never fail. He is called Faithful and True and he is ready to return and gather those who love him.

My prayer is that after reading this book that you know you are never out of God's sight for a second. Whatever you are suffering is before the eyes of God. Remember, *"The LORD is close to the brokenhearted and saves those who are crushed in spirit" (Psalm 34:18).*

Priscilla R. Haley
Author of Broken But God
Visionary of Fearless Faith and God Girlzs with a Vision

Dedication

God spoke to me in prayer a few years ago. He said, "I've given you everything you asked Me for in accelerated time. Now, it's time for you to do My work."

That day I had no idea what He meant, but I knew it was a clear direction to me. As it now unfolds before me each day, I realize that God saved my gift of writing Until Now.

For that reason, Until Now is dedicated to God and God alone. To Him be *ALL* the Glory, *ALL* the Honor and *ALL* the Praise!

I owe You my entire life, Father! May You change the heart and transform the life of every person who is blessed to pick up this book and read it.

I labored in love because You labored with me. Your promises are true, and this is another one for the Kingdom.

Thank You for walking with me and talking with me as I developed this masterpiece.

For Your Glory, Daddy!

Acknowledgments

What would the older me tell the younger me? It's a question I heard years ago, probably on The Oprah Winfrey Show, or a show similar to it. I ask myself that question often. It is one of the reasons why I wrote this book. I acknowledge the younger me who lived life with passion and determination, putting it all on the line for the men she loved and learning all the lessons that come along with that. I also pay homage to every brilliant, beautiful and bold woman who helped to shape me, modeled for me and shared wisdom which helped me dig out of some of the pits of life. I acknowledge these pits because they are where I found my highest strength that created the woman that I have matured into today. In all of my imperfections, there are many times when I got it right. I celebrate those times. I am grateful to my Heavenly Father for being sovereign and for forgiving me so many times and for not leaving me in my ignorance. I acknowledge my future grandchildren and the generations that will come after them for whom I leave this legacy of knowledge and experience.

I hope that some young woman will pick up this book and it will help her make good decisions for her life. I pray that this story will help another sister who has traveled this way heal from the emotional hurt of life's disappointments. I ultimately pray that this work would glorify God's Kingdom and be used to further advance the good news gospel of Jesus Christ. Amen.

Until Now

by

Marcia E. Jackson

I waited patiently
Everything has led up to this moment for me
I held my breath while I waited
Helping the ones I could see
But now it's time
To unwrap the gift
The blessing is in confessing
He loves me
He waited for me
Until Now

"You intended to harm me, but God intended it for good to accomplish what is now being done, the saving of many lives." Genesis 50:20 (NIV)

CHAPTER 1

Meet Taryn

"No matter what a person looks like on the outside, you can never tell their story unless you have lived it with them on the inside, and even then, your experience will be different from theirs." ~ Marcia E. Jackson

Things were not what Taryn expected. She ran her fingers through the front of her brown bang streaked with honey blonde highlights. She moved it from her brow to behind her ear. Sitting on the side of her king size bed, holding her head down, both hands covering her face, she whispered to herself.

"How did I get here?" She had gotten little sleep and she was up crying most of the night. She moved like a snail from the bed to her bathroom mirror to look at herself. Taryn was shaking like a leaf as if she was cold, but she wasn't cold. She was emotionally and spiritually broken. Her lips were chapped and dry. Her eyes were red and puffy and the skin around them was irritated. She splashed cold water across her face as she had seen in the movies to try to wash away the regretful tears.

"I've got to get it together. I've got to get to work." Taryn gave herself a little pep talk as she turned on the shower. She carried the heavy load of her body back to her bedroom where the alarm on her phone chimed. She tapped the snooze button.

"Shoot!" She looked at the time. It was 8:30 a.m. and she was already late for work.

She called her personal assistant, "Good morning Lindsey. Please cancel my morning appointments. I will be in around eleven." She looked over at the mountain of pillows on her bed; her mascara-colored tears had stained one of the pillowcases. The tears gushed uncontrollably from her chestnut brown eyes throughout the night. It bothered her to see the mess, but she couldn't deal with the bed and the pillows in that moment like she wanted to. Plus, she would not want anyone to know she was crying in bed. She decided to let it go, get in the shower to keep focused on getting to work instead.

When she arrived late at her real estate office, wearing sunglasses and dressed in a dark-blue fitted pant suit with a crisp white shirt and pearls, Lindsey noticed her as soon as the elevator doors opened. She followed her into her office.

"Good morning Ms. Madrid! Are you okay?" Taryn simply nodded. "I rescheduled your meetings with Mrs. Taylor and Mr. Davis for early next week. Dreya scheduled lunch for the two of you at noon. This afternoon you have back-to-back meetings with the leadership team here for an update on the Abdullah corporate deal." She stopped mid-sentence. "Are you sure you're okay?"

"Yes, I'm fine, thank you for asking - again. I was just having trouble with my allergies this morning."

Lindsey squinted her eyes through her tortoise-framed glasses. She had worked with Taryn long enough to know when she was hiding something. She also knew when not to press.

She backed away slightly from the desk advancing closer to the door.

Taryn turned her black leather high back chair to look out the window and suddenly swung the chair around throwing up both her hands as if she was fighting with the air. She had looked away because she didn't want her assistant to see the red in her eyes or the lie coming out of her mouth.

Taryn was annoyed that Lindsey had asked if she was okay twice and she didn't want to be bothered with anyone else. "Could you please close the door on the way out and hold all my calls. I need to get a few things done before lunch, and I need to concentrate. Thank you, Lindsey."

"Yes, Ms. Madrid. You're welcome." Lindsey twirled around to leave closing the door behind her.

Taryn grabbed her head and searched her desk drawer for some ibuprofen. She was glad she was able to come up with a lie so quickly. She pulled the mirrored compact from her desk and opened it to take a look at a reflection of herself.

"I look horrible. What in the world was I thinking this morning? My hair and makeup are a mess." Taryn powdered her face, especially under her eyes.

She turned her chair toward the wall of windows and looked out. Off in the distance, she could see the tip of the Capitol building reminding her that she was as close to the seat of political power as one could get. On any other day, she absolutely loved living in the DC suburbs and commuting in to work downtown, but at that moment, from her sunken eyes and ashen look, she appeared empty and hollow. There was no work happening for her at the moment or probably for the entire day. Her growling stomach reminded her that she didn't eat breakfast before leaving the house, so lunch with Dreya would be a much-needed distraction from how she was feeling. It was a few minutes before noon, so she picked up the phone to dial Dreya's office. When she didn't get an answer she said out loud, "I don't feel like being fake with these people right now. Let me stay out of their way." She grabbed her purse and strategically took the long way around to Dreya's office to avoid bumping into her broker or any of her colleagues.

Standing at Dreya's door Taryn mouthed, "You ready for lunch?" Dreya was wrapping up a phone call. She motioned for Taryn to come in and have a seat.

"Ok, thank you. I will. Bye." Dreya hung up her desk phone quickly and gave Taryn her full attention. "Hey lady! That was my agent. I have a big modeling gig this weekend. Then we are gonna par-tay. I hope you can come with me." Dreya stood up, bouncing and shaking her hips side to side as if she was on a dance floor.

Shaking her head, "You've always got something going on. Never a dull moment with you," Taryn chuckled. "You know I can't handle your wild parties, but thanks anyway. You ready to go to lunch?" Taryn redirected the conversation.

"Yes ma'am. I've been wanting to try the new Mexican place that just opened down the street. We can walk if you want to." Dreya pointed in the direction of the restaurant.

"That's fine. Let's do it!" Taryn stood up and walked ahead of Dreya.

At lunch, Dreya questioned Taryn.

"Are you ok, Taryn? Girl, you seem stressed. What's going on?" Dreya leaned forward and stretched her neck, squinting her eyes as if she was able to see right through Taryn.

"Girl, I'll be fine. Just got a lot going on here. I didn't sleep at all last night. You know that corporate real estate deal I've been working on for months with Mr. and Mrs. Abdullah?" Taryn paused for Dreya to respond.

"Yeah!" Dreya nodded and put her elbow on the table, folding her hand under her chin. She appeared interested in hearing about the deal.

"Well it hasn't gone exactly as I planned. Just trying to figure out how to finesse all these egos and keep this thing from completely sinking. Entering this commercial real estate industry is all new territory for me. Sometimes I question whether I can do this." Taryn looked away. It wasn't a total lie, Taryn just wasn't ready to share everything about her personal emotional struggle with Dreya.

"Well don't let it get you down. You've already done more than enough for this company. Girl, you got this!" Dreya assured Taryn she could pull off this deal.

"Yeah, I know. It's just sometimes it feels like I'm spinning my wheels. I've had great success with the company, so far, but I feel like there's more I could be doing. I just don't know what that is," Taryn looked down at her dry cuticles. "I wonder if there's more to life than just a great job and earning money. Don't get me wrong, I love my work and I'm good at it. I don't want to sound like I'm complaining or I'm ungrateful. I'm not. I'm just at a weird place in my life right now."

"Hmmm...I do understand." Dreya appeared unclear on what to say to Taryn. Taryn was usually the one she went to when she had a problem, not the other way around. She looked over Taryn's shoulder at the server holding two plates in the air and she was glad he was headed in their direction.

He placed their food on the table. Taryn ordered the fish tacos and Dreya ordered shrimp quesadillas.

"These both look really good. You wanna share?" Dreya moved her plate within Taryn's reach.

"Sure!" Taryn asked the server for additional plates so they could sample both meals.

They ate their food in awkward silence without saying very much else as Taryn's heavy words had surrounded their table like a shroud. Dreya finally broke the silence.

"This food is the bomb." Dreya slid her fork across the plate to gather the last bite of refried beans and yellow rice.

"Yes ma'am. It was actually quite delicious." Taryn nodded in agreement, licked her lips and pointed to her empty plate.

"This place is definitely now on the list." Dreya looked around at the colorful decorations on the walls and moved her shoulders up and down to the beat of the Latin music playing in the background.

"I sure hate we have to go back to the office, but we both have afternoon meetings." Dreya talked nonstop about her weekend plans as they strolled back to the office.

"Thanks for putting lunch on my calendar. I really needed that." Taryn opened the door to their office building and held it for Dreya to enter.

"You know we wouldn't eat if I didn't make a point of scheduling time for our weekly lunches. I really enjoy them." Dreya pushed the button to the elevator and they got on once the door opened.

They both got off on their floor. "Ok, I'll see you in the meeting this afternoon." Dreya got off the elevator first.

Taryn went back to her office and closed the door. She sat down at her computer to prepare for the update on the Abdullah deal. She poured over the numbers and she held her head in frustration that she couldn't see any way things could work out. She was usually able to see different options. She called Lindsey, who was good with numbers, into her office.

"Can you please take a look at these numbers again? I have to be missing something here." Taryn handed Lindsey the spreadsheet with the itemized costs of closing the deal.

"Sure, I'm on it." Lindsey reached to grab the spreadsheet and walked back to her desk quickly. "You know you have a meeting with them in an hour."

"Yes, I know. Thanks for the reminder," Taryn's tone was sarcastic.

She grabbed the Chinese stress balls sitting on the edge of her desk to try to relieve some of the tension she was feeling. The sound of the balls soothed her for the moment until Lindsey popped back into the room with the spreadsheet about fifteen minutes later.

"I found one area where you may be able to compromise, but it will lower your commission by a significant amount." Lindsey raised her eyebrows when she said commission.

"I was hoping I wouldn't have to go there. Let's keep looking and I will stall them in today's meeting. Taryn grabbed her laptop and the folder she needed for the meeting. It was showtime.

When Taryn arrived in the spacious board room adorned with expensive wood furniture with a wall of windows that overlooked the calm and beautiful Potomac River, her colleagues were choosing their seats. She took the open seat next to Dreya at the oval cherry wood conference table. Dreya was talking to a colleague across the table but stopped to acknowledge Taryn's arrival.

"You good? You got this!" Dreya gave Taryn a quick two thumbs up.

Taryn nodded to acknowledge Dreya's confidence in her. The meeting began and several colleagues provided an update on their projects and deals. Taryn listened for words she could use to stall about her deal when it came time for her to speak.

"Good afternoon everyone. Many of you know I'm working on the Abdullah corporate deal. I want to thank our team of brokers for entrusting me with this important project. I'm still working through the numbers and this deal will be a big win for us, especially in the area of expansion of future corporate deals. I'm looking forward to continuing to work with this client. That's the update for right now." Taryn looked down the table and avoided looking at her colleagues who always asked hard questions.

"Ummm…I was expecting more specifics about the numbers and where we are with the negotiations. What can you tell us about that?" One of Taryn's brokers asked with a wrinkled brow as others around the table shook their heads in agreement.

"Well sir, we are still negotiating. You know it takes a while to get everyone on board. I have a strategy that I'm working, and we are making good progress." Taryn confidently and quickly responded.

"Taryn, this is not like you. You're usually first to report numbers and progress. I'm concerned as it's been months and you don't seem to have a real plan or numbers to close this deal. You should have that by now. As you said, this is a real opportunity for us to branch out into other corporate endeavors. This has to be handled carefully. Are you sure you're up to it?" Taryn's broker looked her directly in the eye.

"I'm absolutely up to it. Do I need to remind you of my stellar work performance that has been proven time and time again by my ability to effortlessly close tough deals? Have I ever let you or the firm down?" She fiddled with her hangnail again. She was nervous but poised.

"No, you have not. This kind of thing is your specialty. That's exactly why we selected you for this one. Let us know if you need support. Let's move on." Taryn's broker went to the next item on the agenda.

Dreya gave her a nod. Taryn was thankful for the professional reputation she had built with the company. It had given her the time she needed to study the deal more to find the answer she was missing. She waited with bated breath for that meeting and the rest of the work day to be over so she could head home to drown in her sorrows.

Before she left work, her broker invited her in to his office for a brief conversation.

"Taryn, you know I have confidence in you, but this is a very important deal. Even though I didn't want to make a big fuss in front of everyone, I have to tell you I am concerned about how you seem to be really relaxed on this one. I don't see that passion and determination that I'm used to seeing in you. What's going on?" He looked Taryn in the eye.

"I just have a lot going on right now. But I can assure you that I'm on it. I just need to get a little rest and I'll be bright-eyed and bushy-tailed tomorrow. You can count on it." Taryn followed with a fake smile before leaving his office.

Plopping down in her chair at her desk, she picked up the folder labeled "Abdullah" and thumbing through the papers inside, she decided to close the deal. She would take the blow to her commission. It wasn't the first time and it wouldn't be the last. She called Lindsey into her office.

"Please call the Abdullahs and let them know these are the final numbers." Lindsey took the folder Taryn was holding out to her and looked at the final numbers.

She gasped, "Are you sure? This is a big hit to your commission. We can keep looking because I'm not sure we can afford this." Lindsey held the folder up and waved it back and forth. She was so dedicated to Taryn that she referenced "we" when mentioning Taryn's commission as if it would impact her paycheck.

Taryn's phone rang. It was Dreya. She was thankful Dreya saved her from having to continue explaining to Lindsey why this was inevitable.

"Hang on a second, Dreya." Taryn put her hand over the phone while she finished speaking to Lindsey.

"Yes, I'm going to have to take the hit on this. Before you leave, please call them and ask what time we can meet next week to sign the paperwork. Thank you, and that's all for today. I'll see you next week. Have a great weekend and please close the door."

Lindsey sang, "Okaaay" as she shrugged her shoulders while pulling the door closed.

"I'm back Dreya, what's up? Taryn swirled her chair around to look out at the lights coming on as it was getting dark.

"Hey! Just checking on you. You wanna have dinner? Me and a few other folks are going to happy hour after work."

"No, I'm gonna head home. I have a few stops to make and I'm really tired. I didn't sleep well last night. I think I'm going to just go to bed early tonight. Thanks, though, and thanks for being my cheerleader today. I needed you and you came through…as always."

"Girl, no problem. That's what friends are for. Get some rest. Hold on." Dreya started talking to someone who entered her office. Taryn hung up before she realized it.

She packed her laptop into her bag and headed for the parking garage. She searched the parking lot for her car. She had been so distracted when she arrived at the office late that morning and because of it, her car wasn't parked in the usual spot. She finally spotted it and walked to her car, got in and drove out of the garage. The sun was starting to set and she opened the sunroof and front windows to let in the fresh air of the Fall evening.

Tears began to form in her eyes and fall down her cheeks as she thought about the day, starting with the morning. Wiping the tears, she drove in silence through the slow-moving rush hour DC traffic out to the suburbs. The traffic was always bad in DC, but today it seemed to take an eternity for her to get out of the city.

She made her first stop at the dry cleaners to pick up her clothes. Taryn searched her console for the dry-cleaning ticket and slowly got out of the car to retrieve her things once she found it. Upon entering the dry cleaners, there was an older man waiting on his clothes with his back to the door. He turned to look at Taryn when the bell on the door sounded after she opened it to enter. He stared Taryn up and down and she could feel his eyes burning a hole through her body while she handed the ticket to the man at the register after he greeted her. Once the dry-cleaning attendant disappeared to find her clothes, the man staring jumped on his opportunity to flirt with her.

"Hello Beautiful! Rough day at work?" The man moved closer to Taryn. She rolled her eyes and snickered as this happened frequently almost everywhere she went. Men loved to flirt with her, especially older men.

"Yes, it was. I'm glad it's over so I can go home and relax." She engaged him even though she just wanted to be left alone. But she also didn't want to seem too mean.

"You live around here?" The female attendant appeared with his clothes and saved Taryn from having to consider how to answer his question.

The man then appeared with Taryn's clothes and she turned her attention to checking her clothes to make sure everything was there. The older man waited until after she was finished checking her clothes. He reached his hand out to give Taryn his business card.

"Why don't you give me a call some time. I'd love to take you out."

"No sir. I can't take your card and you can't take me out but thank you for the offer."

Taryn left him standing there. Amused she could still turn a head or two, even if it was an old head, she quickly opened the door to move on to her next stop.

She drove to her neighborhood grocery store only a few blocks from her house and parked in the closest spot she could find. She prayed out loud.

"Lord, please don't let me see anyone in this store that I know. I can't be bothered right now. I might lose it." She wasn't in the mood for small talk. She pulled herself together enough to get out of the car to grab her favorite items to make home-made veggie pizza for dinner. Homemade pizza with pesto, spinach and mushrooms was her comfort food when she was feeling sad. The background music playing in the store was Whitney Houston's *Where Do Broken Hearts Go?* Listening to the words of the song made the tears gush from Taryn's eyes before she could stop them. She wiped them quickly not want-ing anyone, not even strangers, to know she was in distress as she made her way to the checkout to go home. She got back in her car and drove a few miles to her home.

As she pulled her Mercedes Benz SUV into the 2-car garage, she let out a big sigh. "Finally. Home! Thank You God!" Taryn put the car in park and gathered all her things.

The two-story house was empty and dark. Taryn entered the kitchen through the garage and flicked on the first light she came to. She put down her leather computer bag, the grocery bags and the dry cleaning on the floor next to the island in her kitchen. She stood there in the loud quietness of her clean kitchen for a few minutes. She took a few steps forward and stopped next to the wall leading to her living room.

"What was I thinking? How could I be so stupid? Taryn was reflecting on the day and what her broker had said. "If my boss loses confidence in me, I'm all the way done!" she spoke to the air as she slowly slid down the wall onto the floor. She sat there on the cold, white marble floor seemingly tired and broken.

Taryn had always lived her life to be perfect, which was far from her reality right now. She woke up that morning ques-tioning, "How could a beautiful, educated and accomplished woman like me be in so much pain?"

From the outside, it appeared that Taryn had it all together. She was determined and ambitious. Her family and friends knew it. Once she set a goal, it was only a matter of time before it was done. Like the time when Taryn was in fourth grade, she set a goal to earn all As on her final report card after getting one B all year long in math. She told her mother and grandmother about her goal. She worked hard to accomplish it. When her report card came in the mail after school had let out that summer, she was the first to open the mail with total confidence because she knew she had done it. That was the kind of certainty and determination Taryn lived her life with. She had set very high standards for herself. She was the first in her family to go to college to earn multiple degrees. Her first month in the real estate business, she told her broker her goal was to sell a million dollars in properties the first year and earn the regional award for top sales amongst new agents. In nine months, she had exceeded her goal and earned more than a million dollars in sales. While she had accomplished great things, she was empty. She had lost herself somewhere along the way in life. Fortunately for her, she realized what really mattered most. But by that point, it may have been a little too late.

Taryn took in a deep cleansing breath through her nose. She slowly let it out through her mouth as if that breath would help her make sense of everything that may have been whirling around in her mind. Taryn was a thinker and most times she was a problem solver. More importantly, she was strategic in all her actions. That worked when it came to advancing her career. She knew she could figure out this situation, but at that moment, she looked completely confused and utterly lost. She stood up from the comfy beige couch where she rested after she picked herself up off the floor. She had been sitting there for over an hour staring into space.

"Why God…why?" Taryn yelled. "Why is this happening to me?"

Taryn's cell phone rang jolting her out of the trance. She looked in the direction of the ring, but she didn't move. The phone was still in her purse, which was on the kitchen floor near the island. The evening had turned to night and the streetlights were on. The room was dimly lit with a sliver of light coming in from the streetlight through a tiny opening in one of the beige sheer curtains that hung from the ceiling to the floor. She ignored the phone call, rolling her eyes like she didn't want to be bothered. She slowly walked toward the large bay window in her living room to touch the floor lamp that immediately came on and added soft light to the room. She plopped down in the window seat folding one leg underneath her.

She had spent a lot of time in that window seat. It was one of her favorite places in her living room. It was as if the pillows remembered her and naturally molded to the shape of the weight of her body. No matter what the season, the scenery right outside that window was always beautiful and distracting. Sitting there, anyone could almost forget about whatever it was they were thinking for a moment, whether it was good or bad.

"Well, window, here I am again sitting here with you. I seem to always find my way back here trying to figure out my crazy life." She sat still, took a deep breath in as she looked up to the full moon staring back at her. Something about looking up and seeing the moon and the stars reminded Taryn how deeply connected she was to nature and all human life.

From the time of Taryn's earliest childhood memory, she had a responsibility to stand for good and to be deliberate and intentional about helping others. She had been raised to live a life of excellence. There would be no compromising that in any way.

Taryn rubbed her forehead as if she were trying to focus her attention back to her thoughts. Up to that point in her life, her son, Damon, and his father, Ryan, had been the most significant men in her life, besides her father. Ryan and Damon were responsible for some of her greatest joys and deepest sorrows. Taryn had spent so much of her time over the last twenty years either thinking about them or working on these relationships. She had allowed her life to be dominated by these men and each had shaped who she had become without her really questioning herself about the position each played in her life.

When Taryn first met Ryan, she was a young, naive 18-year-old country girl. They quickly fell in love and married seven years later. Two years into their marriage, Damon was born. It was picture perfect, just what Taryn had shared was her vision for marriage and having kids. Except it wasn't perfect, Taryn and Ryan were married for seven years before their marriage ended in a devastating divorce. She dated a few guys after her divorce, but nothing worth her full attention. Nothing that made her feel the love and passion she first felt for Ryan when they dated and the earlier parts of their marriage.

"Obviously, I'm not good at making decisions about relationships. Clearly, there's a problem." Taryn's tone was one of disgust with herself. She drilled herself, "Was it worth it? Loving and giving so much of myself to Ryan...was it worth it?"

As for Damon, she had worked hard to raise him as a single mom struggling to provide him the opportunities she didn't feel she had as a child. Most times he seemed ungrateful and rebelled against everything that she stood for. It had been exhausting trying to get him to believe in what she wanted for him. Like many mothers, she thought she knew what was best for him. Clearly, she didn't. She often struggled with parenting Damon after the divorce. He wanted to spend more time with his dad than her, even though he lived with her full-time. She had given up so much of herself to make Ryan and Damon happy that she neglected herself.

Taryn hadn't sat that still in a long time. She rubbed her temples. "I know I have the answers. I just have to listen as they come from my heart to my head."

Whatever the answers were, Taryn had come to terms with the reality that it was time to take back her life. She had to stand in her own truth and take back the space that she had allowed Ryan and Damon to take up for the majority of her existence. But how was she to do it? That was the million-dollar question she would have to answer. The two had provided a distraction from the truth that Taryn now had to face.

"Lord, I've given so much to them but how do I take my life back? How do I become whole again?" Taryn looked up at the ceiling like she wanted God to miraculously appear and answer her as she prayed out loud.

This time, Taryn dropped to her knees from the window seat. She sobbed. Her chest and stomach pulsated with each wail. There was no one there to help her understand how the walls of her life had suddenly crashed down.

"The divorce! The disrespect! The lies! How did I not realize I hadn't processed all this mess?" She yelled at God. "Hello! Does yelling get your attention? How did I get here? God, all I ever wanted was a family and now I'm divorced. I have a son who doesn't always take my advice. I know he's trying to figure things out on his own, but it hurts when he rejects my values and everything I've taught him."

Taryn shook her head back and forth as she voiced the painful moments she had avoided dealing with in her adult life. The pain was finally catching up with her and she couldn't run anymore. She couldn't cover it up.

"I have the job I want. I have the house and the car. I have the degrees on the wall. I have the money in the bank, but all of it means nothing because I've lost myself. I can't even seem to enjoy a romantic love relationship because I keep picking the wrong type of guys." It had been years since Taryn had been on her knees before God. She put her face on the clean floor as the cold reality of her life set in deeply in her soul.

"God, I know all this is teaching me something right now. But, I just don't get it. And I know you placed Ryan and Damon in my life to teach me something. God, did I get it? Did I learn what you wanted me to learn?"

The truth was Taryn had learned to love deeply, to pray harder and to trust God when she didn't understand why things happened to her as a result of the significant relationships in her life. Out of the corner of her eye, Taryn noticed a picture taken ten years earlier of her sitting on the beach.

"I had so much fun on that trip." She reminisced as she stared at the picture. "I once had goals. I had my own big dreams. There are desires in my heart that are still unfulfilled.

Maybe now is the perfect time to revisit those." Taryn went over to the picture and picked it up. She lightly touched the image. "I want this version of me back. "God, I admit that I participated in all of this." She wiped away a single tear. "I take responsibility and I am not a victim. God please show me the way out. I promise I will serve you. God, please hear my cry. I need you Lord."

She admitted to God and to herself that she had assumed responsibility for taking care of everybody else, and she had forgotten to take care of herself in the process.

"God, I don't know how to do this. I don't know how to love myself. I don't know how to forgive myself. I don't know how to live with myself." With her shirt sleeve, she wiped the tears draining from her eyes and the mucus from her nose. "I don't know how to pick up the broken pieces of my life. God, I need You to help me! I can't do this without you. Please help me, Father God."

The tears streamed down Taryn's face as she yelled out to the stillness of her spacious house. She stumbled, like a drunk, back toward the window seat. A neighbor was outside staring at her house. That's how loud she was. She didn't care. She needed answers and she knew God was the only one who could provide them.

The phone rang again. Taryn grabbed it to see who was calling. It was her mom, Zoah. Taryn knew she was too insecure and vulnerable in that moment to talk to her mom so she let it go to voicemail. She didn't want Zoah to know she had been living a life filled with shame; shame for allowing Ryan to deceive her in so many ways. Shame for sometimes smothering instead of mothering Damon. Over the years when the burdens of life became too heavy, she would talk to Zoah, about her insecurities, but she would never tell the whole story. She didn't ever want Zoah to worry about her. Living more than a thousand miles away from her family was always hard on Taryn and Zoah. That was also guilt she occasionally let weigh on her. In every one of their conversations, Zoah always reminded Taryn of what she had taught her over the years about having faith in God.

Zoah was a woman of quiet strength and impeccable character. She didn't say much, so when she did speak, Taryn listened. Taryn admired the gracefulness of her mother and aspired to be like her. Zoah was a beautiful woman who stood five feet seven inches with flawless caramel colored skin. She never looked her age and always kept her hair dyed a beautiful honey brown that perfectly matched her butter soft skin tone. Zoah was retired and worked volunteering in her community and in the family church where generations had been raised. The members of that church helped to raise Taryn and her siblings. Because of Zoah, Taryn loved God and she loved helping others. Zoah had instilled both values in her children.

God had done so much in Taryn's life. How dare she question Him. She smiled as she remembered one of her conversations with Zoah...

"Baby, whatever you are going through, God can handle it and He will never leave you. He promised us that. Trust Him. Believe in the word of God. And...you know you can always come home." Zoah laughed as she teased Taryn through the phone. She was always serious about wanting Taryn to come back home. Even after more than twenty years had passed since Taryn moved away.

With a single chuckle, Taryn replied, "I know. I know, Mama. Thank you. I love you." After Taryn hung up from one of their many conversations, she always felt better.

This place was not too deep for God to reach down to grab her. He had done it before. She was firm that God's love is overwhelming and greater than any sin she lived in, dirt she wallowed in, shame she bathed in or turmoil she let into her life.

Taryn hummed the song *Blessed Assurance* as she rocked back and forth.

"Blessed assurance, Jesus is mine." She sang out loud. She sang herself happy and she smiled through the tears.

"His love is greater," Taryn repeated to herself. "God, only Your love can put a smile on my face and a song in my heart. Lord, you are my sun peeking through the clouds after a terrible storm. Once I see that sun, I know the storm is over and everything is going to be okay, even if the cleanup takes some time." Taryn spoke aloud. She would recover yet again even if she had a few battle scars.

Taryn had sat long enough in the window seat. It was well after midnight. She got up to go upstairs and get in bed. She climbed in her king-sized bed that wasn't made from the night before. She flipped the pillow over to avoid the mascara stains.

"I wish I could talk to you right now. I would love to get your insight and wisdom. You would know what to do." Taryn talked to a picture of her and her grandma sitting by her bedside. She took a deep breath. She missed her grandma so much.

Taryn grew up in a tight-knit family and her maternal grandmother had helped to raise her. Grandma Bella had an amazing influence on Taryn's life. She would say things that

Taryn could not understand as a child. But on a day like today, Taryn could finally understand.

One of Grandma Bella's favorite sayings was, "Keep living."

Taryn had experienced enough of life to now understand exactly what that meant; and she chuckled at what Grandma Bella would've done if she saw her looking like a hot mess. She was stretched out all over the floor crying like a spoiled rotten toddler.

Still looking at the picture, Taryn whispered to herself. "Who does that? You would have loved that phrase." She laughed out loud. Her grandmother had the funniest facial expressions. Those facial expressions would've added everything to the moment if she could've been a fly on the wall watching Taryn all day long looking and acting like a desperate wild woman.

Grandma Bella was a rock in Taryn's life and in their family. Taryn looked up to her in every way. She was strong and smart, yet gentle and loving. Grandma Bella lost her mother and father at the tender age of twelve, so she had to make her way in the world to survive. By thirteen, Grandma Bella was married and had started a family. That didn't leave a whole lot of time for her to be formally educated so she only had a third-grade education. Education was everything to her. While she was not formally educated in schools due to her circumstances, she was a wise woman whose life had taught her some especially important lessons about love, family, loss, forgiveness and perseverance. She passed that wisdom and insight on to her children and grandchildren.

"I'm so thankful for everything you taught me while you were here. God, I just wish you were here right now. I know you had to overcome far worse situations than what I'm going through. This would be nothing to you." Taryn talked to the picture like Grandma Bella was sitting right in front of her.

"I know I have to get myself together and I can do this because you survived so much more. And you still managed to give me and everyone you met your very best every day. Lord, I miss you so much." She stared at the picture and admired the beauty of Grandma Bella. The memories of her grandmother's voice, her smile and her infectious laugh must have overwhelmed her because the tears began welling up in her eyes. Taryn couldn't control the fountain of tears that flowed.

There was a time when Grandma Bella got sick and went into the hospital. Taryn didn't immediately head home to Louisiana even though everything in her gut told her to go right then. She was newly pregnant with Damon and having some difficulty with her pregnancy. She was worried and stressed about Grandma Bella's health. She didn't have time to think about her own health or that of her unborn child. Her doctor had ordered her to go on bed rest to prevent a miscarriage. Against her own intuition, she stayed in DC and closely monitored the situation talking to Zoah and other family members often throughout each day.

"She's doing fine. The doctors are going to release her from the hospital in a few days. You don't need to get on a plane right now. Please just stay put Taryn." Zoah reassured her that Grandma Bella would make a full recovery. Ryan was in agreement with Zoah and didn't want Taryn to fly home either.

Taryn agreed not to go as she knew her grandma was resilient in every way and Taryn believed her tenacity and grit for life, her family and her community would carry her through the illness. Taryn was wrong. When she got the call late one night that her grandmother had died, she was completely dev-astated. As soon as Zoah spoke the first word, Taryn knew from the pain in her voice that they had lost her…

"I can't believe she's gone. I knew I should've come home. I knew it. Now I will never be able to see her again." Taryn and Zoah both sobbed on the phone. She was heartbroken.

There was nothing that Ryan or anyone could do or say to console her for days. No one and nothing would ever fill that empty space in Taryn's heart that was created the day Grandma Bella transitioned to heaven.

On a day like the day Taryn had, she became consumed with her grandma. Taryn learned from her grandmother to work hard and make her family proud. She never saw Grandma Bella yell or act out with anyone. Yet, she held a powerful influ-ence in her home and community. She would listen carefully and speak definitively expecting that whatever she said would never be questioned, but would be carried out immediately. It always was. There wasn't a time when she spanked any of the grandchildren in the family, but she used the wisdom of the ages and her faith in God to bring obedience in her offspring.

Her grandmother would say, "Taryn, God is always watch-ing you."

The way she said it was enough to make Taryn and any wayward child who had good sense behave. She was kind and compassionate and she would often help others in the family and in the neighborhood.

Grandma Bella would say, "Make your bed when you get out of it in the morning. A lady does not stay in the bed until noon. She gets up early. Iron your clothes on Saturday for the week. I don't care how late you stay out on Saturday; you better be at church on Sunday morning."

She meant every word she said. These teachings from her grandmother set a foundation on which Taryn built her character and integrity. Hard work, determination, perseverance and discipline were the strong values Grandma Bella made sure her children and grandchildren acquired. Taryn's family didn't have a lot of money growing up, but they always had a lot of love. Taryn had the support of her family cheering her on to victory with anything she accomplished. Family set a foundation for Taryn and gave her the backing to live the life she wanted. For that, she was always grateful.

CHAPTER 2

That Summer

"Life will take us some places that we never thought we would go, and we just have to be ready when we get there." ~ Marcia E. Jackson

The next morning, Taryn was lying underneath the warm, cozy covers with her feet crossed at the ankle. She was rocking her feet back and forth watching the dusty ceiling fan blades spin around over her bed. She was glad it was Saturday and she didn't have to go in to the office. She had stopped working on the weekends years ago. The early morning sun was shining brightly through the sheer beige window panel, and the rays beamed against her face.

"Yesterday was ridiculous and crazy. What was I thinking?" Taryn chuckled at herself under her breath. She arose from the bed, yanked the covers off her legs and threw them off the side of the bed as she stood up.

She raised both arms up over her head standing on her tip toes to extend her stretch even further. Bending her body from left to right, Taryn reached down to touch her toes as she took in a deep breath and let it out slowly as she had done many times in her yoga class.

"I'm hungry. I haven't eaten anything since lunch yesterday." She made a habit of talking to herself as she headed to the kitchen to make herself some breakfast.

"I wonder if Damon came home last night or if he stayed at his dad's house." She grabbed her robe and slid it on over her black spaghetti strap tank top and black boy short underwear before heading down the hall to his room. She pushed the door open and his bed was unmade and empty.

"How many times have I told this boy he needs to clean this room. It's a hot mess in here." Taryn spoke through clenched teeth as she searched the room from top to bottom. There were clothes all over the floor and empty water bottles strewn throughout the room. She looked around like she was tempted to go in and start cleaning. She had done that so many times before.

"You know what…I'm not doing this anymore." She stopped herself from picking up a shirt thrown on the floor. "He has a trash can in here. Why in the world does he not use it? So disrespectful!" She rolled her eyes, closing the door to Damon's room. She walked down the hall to the stairs leading to the kitchen. She shook her head, and her lips were turned up in disgust.

She sat down at the table in her kitchen and looked off in the distance. She grabbed the remote to the 60-inch television mounted on the wall in the family room near the kitchen and flicked through the channels. She stopped to watch a few minutes of SpongeBob Square Pants. It was her favorite cartoon.

She heard the garage door open. A few minutes later Damon appeared in the kitchen.

"Oh, hey mom! How are you?" He was dressed in black and white Nike shorts and a black Nike hoodie. Damon was six feet tall with a slender frame. He wore a size thirteen shoe and he loved playing basketball as much as he loved breathing air. It was one of his favorite things to do with his dad.

"Hey son! I'm good. How are you?" Taryn gave him a hug as he reached over to give her one.

"I'm good! I stayed at Dad's last night. We're about to go play basketball. I came to get my other basketball shoes."

"Oh, okay!"

"What are you doing today?"

"Not sure. Don't have any plans."

You wanna come with us? We'll probably see a movie later."

"Absolutely not! You know I'm not hanging out with your dad." Taryn threw him a look that could kill.

"Okay!" Damon shrugged his shoulders and shook his head as he left the room to head to his bedroom. Taryn followed him.

"Let's talk about your room."

"What about my room?"

"When are you gonna clean it up?"

"Are you serious?"

"Yes, I'm serious!"

"Why do you care about my room?" Damon smirked, rolling his eyes with his back to her so Taryn couldn't see him.

"Because it's in my house," Taryn's hands were on her hips.

"Just close the door and don't come in here," he sucked his teeth.

"I'll come in here whenever I want to. And you need to watch your tone with me." Taryn pointed her finger at Damon.

"Okay Mom, I'm not trying to disrespect you. This is your house."

"It's not just about it being my house. I work really hard to provide a home for us. You have a trash can in your room for a reason. Use it to throw away trash. The bottles all over the floor should be in the trash. Why are they on the floor?"

"Because it's not a big deal to me. I'll pick them up eventually."

"Look, I don't like fussing with you. I don't want any room in this house to look like a trash dump. So, pick the bottles up, put them in the trash and stop putting them on the floor. Problem solved."

"Okay Mom. I will do it when I get back."

"No, you will do it right now before you leave." Taryn wasn't having it. Her nerves were on edge from the minute Damon asked her to hang out with him and his dad.

"But I've got to go. Dad's waiting on me."

"And he can wait for you to pick up these bottles."

"Okay, you win." He threw his hands up in concession. Damon picked up the bottles and put them in the trash. When he finished, he grabbed his sneakers from the closet and rushed past Taryn.

Taryn yelled as he disappeared through the kitchen into the garage. "And make sure you come home tonight so you can get your clothes and the rest of this stuff off the floor."

Damon didn't answer. Taryn was heated. She heard the garage door close. She sat down in the kitchen to calm down and finish watching television.

Her cell phone was sitting on the table next to her. It rang. She didn't look away from the television. The phone rang again, and she looked down at it. The Caller ID read, "Socar McAllister." Taryn picked up the phone but decided not to answer. Socar had been trying to reach her since the night before.

'I'm not ready to talk to anyone yet. I can't right now." Taryn mumbled and put the phone face down turning the volume down to silence the phone.

The doorbell rang. "Ugh, who could that be? I didn't order anything." Taryn got up and peeked out the window. Socar was staring back at her and waving.

"Shoot!" Taryn had no other choice but to open the door.

Socar McCallister was twenty years an elder to Taryn, and she had been her mentor for more than two decades. Taryn looked down at herself, ran her fingers through her hair to try to smooth it down and wrapped her robe around her tightly shaking her head in shame while opening the door.

"Hey there, what brings you to the neighborhood?" Taryn mustered up a smile and reached out to hug Socar as she stepped through the front door.

"Where have you been? I've been calling you since last night. I was worried about you. Are you okay?" Socar walked past Taryn into the living room looking around the house as if she could find the answer to her question.

Socar was dressed to kill. She was always impeccably dressed. It didn't matter whether she was running to the store or going to a show and dinner. She was what one would call a supreme diva. When it was cold outside, you could catch her in her full-length mink coat. While most women her age were wearing shoes for comfort, Socar wore five to six-inch heels and she had a designer shoe and wardrobe collection that Taryn admired and envied.

"I'm okay, I just needed a minute to myself." Taryn closed the door and followed Socar to the living room. She plopped down on the couch facing Socar who was sitting in her favorite oversized chair. She sat in the same chair every time she visited Taryn.

"What's wrong hunni? You don't look good." Socar examined Taryn. "Your eyes are all puffy. Your hair is all over your head. Your stuff is all over the floor in the kitchen. It's noon and you're still not dressed on this gorgeous Saturday." She took a breath. "This is not like you at all. Have you been crying all night?" Socar got up and moved to the couch. She stared into Taryn's eyes waiting for her to answer.

"No, I'm not okay. I haven't been okay in a while." Taryn looked down at a spot on the marble floor. She rubbed her eyes like she was trying to rub out tears.

"Well, what's wrong?" Socar put her hand on Taryn's back to encourage her to share what was bothering her.

"Who was I before I was someone's girlfriend, someone's wife, a mother?" Taryn looked up at the ceiling as if the answers would fall from the sky.

"What do you mean?" Socar was shaking her head back and forth.

"I feel like I've lost myself. I've been so busy." She paused. "To look at me...yeah...people think I've got it going on." Taryn snapped her fingers in the air three times to make her point. "But...I'm not so sure what I've accomplished is truly what I wanted from my life." Taryn was real with herself and Socar for the first time.

"Oh sweetie! Is that all?" Socar asked with raised eyebrows. "You're not the first woman to ask these questions? Do you know how many women before you have had to search for the answer to these questions once they become wives and mothers?" Socar reassured Taryn.

"Okay, but I don't know what to do now. I don't know what to do with how I'm feeling. I usually know how to control my life. How do I turn things around?" Taryn couldn't lie to Socar. She would read Taryn like a book. That's one of the reasons Taryn loved her.

"Child...if I got paid every time I've asked myself these questions over the last sixty years of my life, I would be a wealthy woman." Socar sat back on the couch and kicked her shoes off.

"Hunni you will figure that out and it will change as you change. I've had to trace my life back to the beginning to understand where I am today. You may have to do the same. When was the last time you felt like yourself?" Socar moved back to the chair and put her feet up on the ottoman.

"You got anything to drink around here?" Socar raised one hand as she knew Taryn needed to talk but she wanted her favorite iced peach tea. Taryn always kept her tea on hand for whenever she dropped by.

"Yes, of course I do." Taryn got up and went to the kitchen, put ice in a glass and poured the tea. She walked back into the living room and handed it to Socar.

"Thank ya hunni! Now take me back...where did you lose yourself?" Socar sipped her tea slowly making a slurping sound with her lips.

"Well, I would have to go back to that summer after high school graduation. That was a critical point for me." Taryn stared off into space. "It was the first time I can recall that I was only responsible for myself. I remember feeling free that summer. It was as if the whole world was available to me. I was about to start college in the fall, and I felt confident that my plan to continue my education at a school about an hour away was a good one."

Taryn put her feet up on the couch and smiled widely as she continued. "My family was so proud of me. The ladies at my church helped me complete my college application and they had been there for me every step of the way. I distinctly remember Ms. Franklin who was extremely helpful in getting me accepted to college. I can still remember that day…"

"Taryn, what are you going to do after high school?" Ms. Franklin asked one Sunday after church service.

"I'm going to college and I'm going to study business." I responded proudly and confidently to Ms. Franklin's question.

"Good girl!" Ms. Franklin would shake her head up and down while peering over the top of her black cat eye shaped reading glasses connected to a silver chain around her neck.

"We all know someone like Ms. Franklin. Mine was Ms. Turner." Taryn and Socar both laughed.

"I was so proud to be going off to college." She stood up as she noticed Socar's glass was empty. Socar always drank two glasses of tea and Taryn yelled to continue her story from the kitchen until she returned with the tea and gave it to Socar.

"Thank you darling! Tell me more about Ms. Franklin." Socar put the second glass of tea up to her mouth and took a small sip.

Taryn delightfully indulged her. "Ms. Franklin was an educator who watched me grow up in the church. She taught me about God and the Bible. I went to Sunday school every Sunday and Vacation Bible School every summer. Ms. Franklin and several other ladies who worked with the youth expected all of the children at Mount Calvary Baptist Church to excel and she and the other pushed us all to go to college."

"I never questioned whether going to a four-year college after high school made sense. It was what my friends were doing, and I knew it was what my family expected of me. At least that was how I interpreted the messages I got from the influential people in my family. I can still remember conversations with my mom, Zoah, and my Grandma Bella…"

"'Get your education so you never have to depend on anyone to take care of you.' That's what my mother, Zoah, told me."

"My Grandma Bella backed my mother's words. She would say, 'Taryn, once you get your education, no one can take it away from you.' "Her words echo in my head to this day."

Taryn looked over at a picture of her mom and grandmother on her fireplace mantle.

"I watched my mom study after she went back to school to earn her accounting degree. For me, watching my mom was a model of the importance of obtaining an education. My mom is a giant in my life…all five feet, seven inches of her. She was always a beautiful woman with her caramel colored skin and quiet and gentle spirit. She was completely dedicated to raising me and my sister and brother. She sacrificed everything for us, making sure we had everything we needed and a lot of what we wanted. My mom made it look easy, but I know today more than ever, that it wasn't easy raising three children as a single mother. She relied on my Grandma Bella and other family members for support with raising us."

"What about your dad? What was his influence in your life?" Socar delved deeper into Taryn's family.

"My dad, Evan, is six feet four inches tall, dark and handsome. His baritone voice is distinct, and he never had to repeat himself twice with me. He's a gentle giant and I respect him and appreciate all that he has done for me. He also believed in education and he took every opportunity to make it known. He would say, 'Taryn, as long as you're going to school and doing what you're supposed to do, I'll support you.' And he always did…"

Taryn stood up and walked over to the window and looked out at the leaves changing colors on the trees as she added to her response to Socar's question. "It was clear to me that obtaining my education would make everyone proud. Earning a college degree after high school was also something that few others in my family had done and it was just the kind of challenge that fed my need to achieve. I love learning, and the thought of going away to college thrilled me."

"You mentioned the summer after high school being a significant time in your life. What was going on that made that time so important to you?" Socar reminded Taryn how the conversation started.

"After I graduated from high school, I was meeting new people and developing my sense of independence. I was also very impressionable and completely naïve. Everything was new to me as my world had opened up considerably. I had just turned eighteen a month before graduation and my dad gave me his black Jeep as a graduation gift. I was ready to roll. I remember the day my dad gave me that car. My dad lived in Texas so he drove it to my mom's house and gave it to me after my graduation ceremony…"

"Congratulations baby, I'm so proud of you." Evan said to Taryn holding the keys to her Jeep by the key ring as they dangled in front of her.

"Are you serious right now? Thank you, Dad!" Taryn reached for the keys and hugged Evan tightly as she rested her head on his chest for a moment.

"I'm giving you this car as I promised. You must take care of it. Call me if anything goes wrong. Don't just let things go, but let me know immediately if something needs to be fixed." Evan told her as Taryn looked up to him, still locked in an embrace.

"Ok, Dad! I will." Taryn promised Evan.

"Also, slow down, Taryn. Don't get any tickets driving up and down that road in this car. The insurance is already high enough and you don't have a job." Evan warned Taryn with his proud smile and a raised eyebrow as he gave her a slight chuckle.

"Alright Dad, I won't." Taryn eagerly gave Evan back a wide smile. He was known for giving long speeches, but she was hoping it wasn't so bad that day. She was ready to look inside her new car…

Taryn sighed deeply. "That was a wonderful time in my life." Taryn sat back on the couch next to Socar and shared more about her family.

"I would've agreed to just about anything my dad said at the time. I really wasn't listening. I was too excited about having my own set of wheels. My mom and dad weren't together, but he only lived a few hours away. He wasn't there to monitor me with the car directly, so he gave me and my mom a list of important things to know about owning the car. He and my mom did a wonderful job-sharing responsibility for raising me even though they were no longer in a relationship. She took on the responsibility for helping me learn how to drive the car, even though she didn't know how to drive it herself. The Jeep had a manual transmission. It wasn't long before I figured it out."

"Wait! Your dad gave you the keys and you didn't know how to drive a stick shift?" Socar asked confused.

"Yup! He sure did. It was all mine. I couldn't move the car, but I was determined to learn how to drive it because I had places to go. Once my dad's friend picked him up I got in and checked the car out."

"Boy, he must've really trusted you. Okay, so how did you learn how to drive the car?" Socar was smiling from ear to ear waiting to hear more.

"Mom and I went to the parking lot of my high school. I drove the car for hours until I got the hang of balancing the clutch and the gas pedal with shifting the gears." Taryn shifted her feet and moved her right hand back and forth as if she was driving the car.

She continued, "Mom could only provide encouragement because it had been a long time since she had driven a stick shift car. It meant everything to me to have her there. I remember there was a little hill by the house on our way back home and I must have spent more than an hour trying to climb it to get us home. It felt like I was going to blow the transmission trying to master that little hill. Mama said...

"Taryn, take your time honey, you can do it."

"Come on. I can do this." I was talking myself into it, while I took deep breaths. Then I got it! I slowly let up off the clutch and pressed the gas to climb the hill. I screamed, "Yes, I did it." I pressed the gas and accelerated up the hill.

"Yes, you did." My mom celebrated but boy she breathed a huge sigh of relief. Taryn pumped her fist as she and Socar celebrated. "I felt a great sense of accomplishment that day and I was ready to roll in my new car. Right after that I joined mom in the kitchen where she was making dinner to let her know that I was ready to go out and style and profile in my new car...

"Mama, I'm going out tonight to a party and I'm planning to drive my car." Taryn looked over Zoah's shoulder to see what was in the large silver pot she was stirring.

"Are you sure you're ready, Taryn? It's only been one day since you learned how to drive it." Zoah stopped what she was doing to look directly at Taryn.

She could see the concern on her mother's face. "I know Mama, but I've got to get out there some time. I might as well do it now." Taryn hunched her shoulders and threw her hands in the air.

"Well, I guess you're right. Please be careful." Taryn was responsible so Zoah trusted her to be safe.

"I will." Taryn turned and walked away relieved she didn't have to convince her mom any further to let her drive her car to the party.

"I was so excited. I loved that car. I put over two hundred and fifty thousand miles on that car before I donated it to a local charity." Taryn looked up and nostalgically smiled as Socar watched her face light up with a smile.

"Once I got my wheels, it was on. Me and my best friend, Lisa, had plans every weekend. Lisa was a beautiful coffee, with a little cream, colored southern belle with chiseled facial features strong enough for her to take the leading role in any Hollywood movie. Her beauty was often admired by those of the opposite sex and deeply envied by females who didn't know her. Lisa knew she was beautiful, but she never let it get to her head. She was always grounded and humble. We would make our plans and it would go something like this…"

"Hey girl! Are we going out tonight?" Taryn called Lisa while she painted her nails.

Lisa always answered her phone when Taryn called because she knew it was about a party or something fun.

"Yup, you know it!"

"What time do you want to get together?"

"Let's get together about 9 or 9:30."

"Ok, sounds good! See you then…"

"And our plan for partying would be in motion." Taryn threw her hands up in the air in front of Socar and moved her shoulders up and down as if music was playing.

"Lisa and I went to the same high school and our birthdays were both in April. We also went to the same college and we shared a room. We had so much fun at Louisiana Tech University. We couldn't wait to get on that campus and decorate our room. We had big dreams of finishing college and living a great life in a big city other than where we grew up. That summer, Lisa and I did everything together. One night, we went to a party and that's where everything changed. That was the first time I met Ryan.

"Oh really! I don't think you ever told me how the two of you met." Socar interjected.

"You're right! Now that Damon is about to graduate high school, I've been thinking a lot about that summer when we met. Here's to a trip down memory lane…"

CHAPTER 3

Being His Wife

*"Own every part of your life. The good, the bad and espe-
cially the ugly, for it is where you find your inner strength,
beauty and God's amazing grace." ~ Marcia E. Jackson*

The lights were turned up in the room and the music stopped.
The party was over, and it was time to leave. Taryn scanned
the room for Lisa who had been missing for a minute.

"Now, where is she?"

Taryn had a big smile on her face now that she could actually see all the people she had mingled with and the men she
had flirted with for hours at the party that evening.

Lisa had disappeared shortly after they arrived. Taryn knew
what that meant. She met someone. For the time she had been
missing in action, whoever he was, Lisa really liked him.

"There you are." Taryn found Lisa with her back up against
the wall in a corner talking and laughing with a guy. She walked
over to them.

One thing immediately stood out to Taryn about this guy.
He was of Asian descent. He was average height and build and
very handsome. He had a thin face with long dimples that ran

from his cheekbone down to his lower jaw along both sides of his face. His eyes lit up when he smiled, and his teeth were glistening white. Taryn wasn't surprised that Lisa had spent her time that night getting to know him. They had talked about dating men outside of their race and while Taryn hadn't ever imagined herself dating anyone other than a black man, Lisa was open to exploring relationships with men from different races.

Lisa grabbed Taryn by the hand and pulled her toward her with one arm around her neck in a half embrace as she introduced Taryn.

"John, this is my girl, Taryn." Lisa leaned forward toward John in a playful way.

"How are you? It's good to meet you, Taryn." John replied, looking back and forth between the girls.

Taryn did a three second head to toe assessment of John to check him out. Lisa had quickly become comfortable with John by the wide Cheshire cat smile on her face when she leaned in closely to talk to him even though the music had stopped. John was definitely feeling her too as he shared how much he enjoyed the night with Lisa. He complimented the DJ and shared his interest in music and DJing on occasion.

"What's up?" Ryan appeared from behind Taryn and gave her a head nod. He greeted John with a closed fist pound.

"You ready to go man?" Ryan appeared impatient and even a little rude as he pressed John about leaving.

John ignored Ryan's aggressive behavior and introduced Taryn and Lisa to Ryan.

"Hey Ryan, I want you to meet my new friends, Lisa and Taryn."

Ryan extended his hand to shake Lisa and Taryn's hands before turning away as he said, "It's nice to meet you both. I'm ready to get out of here man."

Ryan was constantly looking over his shoulder and looking around the room.

"Are you looking for someone? Or is someone looking for you?" His behavior screamed for Taryn to playfully ask him. Ryan just looked past Taryn and didn't answer her.

Taryn didn't notice anything special about Ryan and it wasn't an instant love connection for her. Ryan was cute, but not the kind of man that would catch her eye. Ryan had milk chocolate smooth skin with short black wavy hair. He was overly confident and a bit cocky as they all moved toward the door to leave. John walked Lisa to Taryn's car, and they exchanged phone numbers. As soon as Lisa and Taryn pulled away, John called Lisa.

"Wow, someone's eager to keep talking." Taryn teased Lisa. She was glad they made a connection.

They talked the whole way as Taryn drove through the city. About fifteen minutes later, she pulled into Lisa's driveway to drop her off at home and they were still talking.

"I'll see you later. Let me know when you get home." Lisa opened the car door to get out.

"Yep, I'll call you when I get home. If you don't answer, I'll know why." They both laughed.

Taryn called Lisa when she got home. There was no answer as she predicted. She drifted off to sleep.

Lisa called Taryn later that morning and woke her up. "Hey, sorry I missed your call. John had me on the phone until the sun came up. I'm surprised I'm up right now." Lisa was her bubbly self.

"You must really like him to stay on the phone all that time. What did y'all talk about?" Taryn was curious.

"Girl, everything! It was so easy to talk to him. On the outside, we look so different. But as we started talking, we have a lot in common."

When Lisa and John wanted to get together later that day, Lisa asked Taryn for a ride to meet John. She mentioned that Ryan would be there.

"Hey, what are you doing later today?" Lisa and Taryn were making plans for the evening after their laughs about the people in the club the night before.

"I don't really have any plans. Why, what's up?" Taryn was open to doing something later.

"I wanna go see John. We talked about getting together later today and maybe doing something tonight. He's a nice guy. His friend, Ryan, from last night will be there too." Lisa threw that in to convince Taryn.

"Oh, ok, I don't really remember him. Was he the guy that acted like someone was looking for him? He was weird." They both laughed.

"Yes, that was him. Maybe he will be a little more focused today. Don't know what was up with him." Lisa acknowledged she also noticed Ryan was distracted.

"Ok girl, I don't have anything else to do this evening. Why not?" They made plans to see the fellas later that evening...

Socar interrupted Taryn. "This seems like it's going to be a long story and I'm definitely interested in hearing it. But before you go on, I'm hungry. We've been sitting here for a while and it's time to eat something. You look like you could use some food too. Do you want to order something, go out or are you cooking?"

"Well, I was about to cook something when you came over. But I'm really feeling like I could get out of this house right now. It's such a beautiful day. Why don't I shower, put on some clothes and we can go out? Give me a few minutes. I'll make it quick."

Taryn ran upstairs, jumped in the shower and reappeared in twenty minutes with her New Orleans Saints hat covering her hair that was pulled back into a ponytail, wearing her favorite black sweat pants and hoodie and black and gold Ugg boots. The Fall weather was just perfect for her outfit.

"I'm not as fly as you, but this will have to do right now." Taryn laughed as she opened the front door for Socar.

"Please! You don't have to be like me. Just be comfortable with who you are." Socar was always teaching Taryn.

They jumped in Socar's convertible Jaguar and buckled their seatbelts. Socar backed out slowly and headed down the road.

"Let's go to Georgetown. I'm thinking Sequoia's. They have a nice brunch." Socar looked at Taryn to see if she was in agreement.

"Sounds good to me."

"Since we have a little drive to the city you can finish telling me the story. Did you have a change of heart about Ryan?"

"No, not immediately. He kinda grew on me..."

"Later that evening when we arrived at John's apartment, it was obvious that he was a sports fan. There was New York Knicks and New York Giants sports paraphernalia all throughout his apartment. John was from New York and Ryan was from Washington, DC..."

"Somebody is a huge sports fan." Lisa smiled and picked up some of the sports items on John's coffee table.

"Yep, I got most of these attending games with my dad up north in New York." John pointed to different items as he shared stories with the three of them.

Ryan chimed in boasting about his love for the Washington Redskins football team.

"Man, one of the best teams in the NFL right now is the Redskins. They're the team to beat. Hey Taryn, maybe you could come home with me to visit DC and go to a game." Ryan was sure of himself and touched Taryn's arm when he spoke to her.

"Um, we just met, so we'll have to see about that. How about we get to know each other first." Taryn fired back with a smile to let him know he wasn't that cute, and she wasn't that easy.

Taryn pulled her hat down tightly as the wind lifted it as they were riding along. She continued talking to Socar.

"From that first date, the four of us became inseparable for the last month of the summer before we started college. John and Ryan were both working for a computer tech company and they were in the area doing work to build the computer networking infrastructure. They were both at least five years older than me and Lisa so they had the money to take us on double dates where most guys our age couldn't. We loved it."

"I bet y'all did. Thinking y'all were grown and all." Socar gave Taryn the side eye as she shook her head.

"That Fall, when we started college about an hour away, Ryan and John would make plans to meet up mid-week and on weekends to be with us. We would travel to see our guys even on weekdays and sometimes, at the expense of our schoolwork. Neither of us were balancing work and play, and we both had a semester where our grades suffered..."

"We've got to get it together. My mama is gonna be so disappointed in me." Lisa was looking at her grades on her computer screen.

"Yea, this has not been the best semester for me either." Taryn plopped down on her bed, biting her lip.

"So, what did you all do?" Socar gripped the steering wheel and looked over her left shoulder before she changed lanes to get around a car stopped in front of her.

"We both realized we needed to prioritize our education. We buckled down on our studies from then on. We limited our time with the fellas to the weekends. We both continued to date John and Ryan throughout our college years. John had already proposed to Lisa that first year of college, but they waited to get married until after graduation. They moved to Texas and immediately started their family and raised three children."

"And you moved here to be with Ryan?"

"Yes! Ryan moved back home to DC the summer before my last year of college. We continued our long-distance relationship until I graduated. A few days after graduation, I packed all my belongings and moved here to begin my new life with Ryan.

"Aw! What you describe seems picture perfect." Socar navigated through the city traffic to South Capitol Street onto Maine Avenue past the Washington monument and the King, Jefferson and Lincoln memorials to make her way uptown to Georgetown.

Taryn kept talking. "It was picture perfect. If only things had gone exactly as we had planned. Two years passed and Ryan and I settled into our life together. I found work in a small minority business and Ryan was a successful computer network engineer. Our lives were perfect, yet one thing was missing…the ring."

Socar laughed, "You are so dramatic."

I consistently asked him, "When are we getting married?"

Ryan would always respond the same way, "When I ask you."

"When are you going to ask me?"

"When I'm ready."

"The conversation went the same way every time we had it. For those few years, I was really frustrated. I was also getting pressure from my family back home to get married. My dad was especially vocal about his disapproval of us living together. Every time I felt the weight, I would put the pressure on Ryan. That's why I will never forget the day Ryan finally proposed to me."

"It was in mid-August and a marriage proposal was the farthest thing from my mind that day. We were having a cookout at our house to celebrate summer as we usually did with our family and friends. Our house was the party house where people regularly gathered to reconnect, refresh and renew themselves. We were both social butterflies and we enjoyed entertaining and having people over. It didn't matter if it was the holidays, football games, or just a typical weekend, our motto was, the more the merrier. People were always welcome in our home."

"This sounds perfect for a proposal. Keep talking…I always enjoy a good love story."

"Yes, it was perfect. My mom and some other family members were in town visiting, so Ryan had planned his proposal perfectly. I totally appreciated the thoughtfulness that went into everything so that my mom and family could witness the proposal. I was busy filling empty dishes with more food when Ryan called me to the pool area in front of everyone and grabbed my hand. Ryan's friend, Zach, was DJ'ing the party. He had stopped the music while Ryan made a speech about how much he loved me and wanted to spend the rest of his life with me. By the time I realized what was happening, Ryan was down on one knee with tears rolling down his cheeks and Zach was playing *Let's Get Married* by Al Greene. It was so unexpected that day even though we had discussed the topic of marriage several times."

"I guess he was ready, huh?"

"Well, you could say that. Unfortunately, he didn't have all the pieces to put the marriage puzzle together. And neither did I."

"Most people don't. That's why so many marriages end in divorce."

"Exactly! We were married within six months of the proposal. It was a fairy tale wedding. Me and a few of my close friends that I had met in DC traveled back to my hometown in Louisiana to meet up with some of my close friends back home, and we had a fabulous time. Ryan's family and close friends also joined us for our nuptials. The wedding took place on an absolutely perfect day in September. We were so happy. Before the reception, we snuck away to our honeymoon suite to consummate our marriage. I've chased that intimate moment a thousand times in my dreams. I'll never forget how good it felt to finally be his wife…"

"Hello, Mrs. Madrid." Ryan whispered lovingly in Taryn's ear as he kissed her neck softly and they both fell on the bed still fully clothed in their wedding garments.

"Hello, Mr. Madrid." Taryn playfully responded to him as she looked him in the eye, caressed his head and invited him to kiss her more.

"We had made love before, but this time was different. Now that we were man and wife, I finally could make love to Ryan without feeling guilty as I had in the past. I was free to fully enjoy this intimate experience with my husband. I looked forward to many more nights of sweet love making."

"Yes ma'am! I do understand." Socar raised shouting hands like she did in church and they both laughed out loud.

"We returned to the wedding party and we danced the night away with our family and friends. We enjoyed every moment of our special day. The next morning, we headed to Cancun to enjoy a weeklong honeymoon."

"Sounds amazing!" Socar drove into the parking garage and whipped her car into the first vacant spot. She and Taryn got out and walked toward the restaurant.

"It was amazing!" Taryn looked around, "It's been a while since I've been to Georgetown. A lot has changed."

"Yes, it has. It's happened all over the city. DC is no longer the Chocolate City we knew and loved back in the day."

"Ain't that the truth. In the twenty years that I've been here, I've seen a lot of changes."

They arrived at Sequoia's restaurant which sat on the edge of the Potomac River in historic Georgetown. The sun was shining brightly reflecting beautifully off the water. The water was still and calm as there was almost no wind blowing to disturb it.

"Wow! I forgot how beautiful this view is. They've done quite a few renovations in here too. This all looks new." Taryn pointed out the chic, upscale, modern interior design that perfectly matched the swanky ambience of the restaurant.

"Apparently, a few other folks had this place in mind for brunch. Let's see if we can get a table. Excuse me…a table for two please." Socar stepped up to the hostess area.

"Right this way ma'am." The hostess immediately found a table with two chairs by the window that gave them a breathtaking view of the Potomac River and the boats that were docked there.

As they took their seat, Socar and Taryn looked at the plates of food to help them decide what they wanted.

The waitress came over and took their drink order and asked if they would be having the brunch buffet or ordering from the menu.

"I'm good with the buffet. It looks like it has everything I want. What about you, Taryn?"

"Works for me! I've been looking at the plates and I definitely want to try some of what I see. So, let's do it."

The waitress explained how the buffet service worked. She pointed out the waffle and omelet station, fresh fruit, pastries, breakfast items, cold and hot food, seafood, desserts of all kinds and invited them to dig in and enjoy.

"You go first, and I will watch our purses." Socar stood up and placed the cloth napkin that was sitting in her lap on the back of her chair.

"Sounds good. Now where is that omelet station?" They both laughed.

When Taryn returned and they both had their food and drinks Socar was ready to hear more.

"So, what happened to you and Ryan? It seemed like things got off to a good start. Where did things start to go wrong for you two?"

"Ha!" Taryn chuckled. "I'll tell you where things started falling apart…"

"As the years rolled by and we adjusted to married life, I realized I was clueless about what it meant to be Ryan's wife. I was woefully unprepared to take on that responsibility. From the time I was a little girl, I had learned from the significant women in my life that having a man was extremely important to my happiness and well-being. I put a lot of weight on the messages I received about the importance of being attached to a man, sometimes even at my own expense. Grandma Bella would say…"

"You need to be able to cook and keep a clean house in order to keep a man happy, Taryn."

"So, I made sure I kept a meal on the table and the house clean, even though Ryan didn't seem to care about any of those things. I still did them because that was what I had been taught was important to having a healthy marriage. One time I had eavesdropped and listened in on my mother and her friends as they had girl talk about how to keep a man happy so that he would be convinced to marry. One of the women said…"

"Girl, put that thang on him and he won't be able to resist." They laughed after they had each had a few glasses of wine.

I didn't know exactly what that meant but I drew some conclusions from their conversation about what it meant, and I always made sure I kept myself beautiful and sexy for Ryan. I let down my inhibitions in the bedroom and I was willing to try just about anything to keep Ryan happy. It didn't stop him from visiting strip clubs every Friday night, though. That was his routine with his friends and he and I argued about it often."

"When we argued about it, Ryan would vehemently say, 'I go to play pool with the fellas. It's not about the women and it's not about you, Taryn.'

"Wow! He definitely did not understand very much about you as his wife to say something like that."

"Right! At first, I tried not to think about it, but as each week came to an end, I became more anxious because I knew where Ryan would be spending his Friday night. He would be out until the wee hours of the morning. I was insecure to know that my man would rather look at strange naked women in a club instead of spend time with me. It didn't feel right and I felt helpless to change his mind. It went against the intimacy I valued in our marriage. One time, I remember starting a conversation with Lisa when I was brave enough to share a little of what was going on with Ryan…"

"Girl pick your battles. Let him know you want to go out with him on Friday night and plan something fun for the two of you to do together. Redirect his focus. You can do it!"

"Ok, I'll try it. Thanks girl." Taryn hung up with Lisa and waited for Ryan to get home.

She heard Ryan come in and greeted him with a kiss when he walked through the door.

Hey, how was your day? You want some dinner?"

"No, I'm good. Thank you." Ryan headed toward the bedroom. Taryn followed him.

"Hey, Ryan, let's plan to go out this Friday night. There's a new movie that I want to see. Maybe we could double date with another couple."

"Taryn, you know that's my time with the fellas. We can go to the movies Saturday night," Ryan looked at her with a look of frustration on his face.

"I don't understand why you are unwilling to budge on this issue." She continued in on him.

"You know what…I'm so tired of arguing with you, Taryn. Do you want to come to the club with me?"

"Are you serious? Ok, yea, let me come with you to see why you can't seem to stay away from this place because I just don't understand it…"

The waitress interrupted Taryn's story, "Can I get you all anything else?"

"No, we're fine. Thank you. You can bring the check, please."

Socar was eager to know what happened next.

"Please don't tell me you went with him."

"I did."

"That wasn't a good move for you and definitely not for him."

"Nope. But I wanted to see what was going on that he just could not stay away from that place."

"Had you ever been to a place like that?"

The waitress appeared again. Socar took the check from the waitress and slid her credit card that was already in her hand inside the cover without even looking at the bill. She handed it back to the waitress without blinking or taking her eyes off Taryn.

"Sure, there were a few times I had gone to see male strippers with my girlfriends. I went to try to make Ryan jealous. It never worked. He didn't seem to care. He even encouraged me to go. Deep down, I never needed this kind of sexual experience to fulfill me. I was happy being Ryan's wife and making love to him as often as we chose to."

The waitress brought the paid bill back to the table and thanked them, "Please come see us again."

Socar opened the front cover and took her credit card out and put it back in her purse.

"Thank you for brunch. I appreciate it."

"You're welcome! You ready to go?"

They both stood up and walked toward the front door of the restaurant. The sun kissed both their faces as they stepped outside.

"It's such a beautiful day. You wanna walk off some of this food?" Socar rubbed her stomach.

"Sure! I definitely need to move some of this food around."

"I don't want to pry, but I really want to know what happened when you went to that place?"

Taryn laughed at Socar. "You're usually the one telling the story and I'm usually the one listening. It's funny to me, but I will continue with the story."

"When we walked into the club, Ryan was immediately greeted by name as he was a regular. Ryan was always social, and I was sure he was no different when he was there."

"Hey Ryan!" one slender brown-skinned woman said in a flirtatious way as she waved to Ryan.

The lacy garment she wore was held together by a few strings at her neck and tied around her waist. It barely covered her breasts and vaginal area and her butt was totally exposed.

Ryan waved back with a smile on his face as he avoided making eye contact with me. He felt me give him a death look with squinted eyes, but he still responded.

"Hey Cinnamon."

I looked at Ryan with a raised eyebrow to confirm his discomfort. He grabbed my hand and we continued walking through the club to the back where the pool tables were. We passed the stage where a woman was completely naked and dancing around a pole that stood in the middle of the stage. Ryan's friends were waiting for him at the pool table when we got there. They were pissed that he brought me, and they let him know it. Those busters said..."

"Oh, my God, Ryan, why did you bring her here?" Ryan's friend, Charles, yelled across the room when he saw the two of them heading over.

"Man, I had to." Ryan sheepishly responded.

"What's wrong? Oh, you don't want me to see you up in here, Charles?" Taryn walked over to Charles to get a better look at him in the eye. "Are you ashamed?" She was now in his face with her head tilted to one side and pursed lips.

"No, I'm not ashamed, you're just not supposed to be here." Charles said shaking his head back and forth looking at Ryan like he wanted to kill him.

"Well, I'm here." Taryn laughed. "And I may just start coming all the time since y'all seem to think it's okay for *MY HUSBAND* to be here every Friday night." Taryn looked accusingly back and forth at Ryan's three other friends, Percy, Dave and Ken. The three of them were standing around the pool table in silence with their pool sticks chalk side up like three young boys being chastised by their mother.

"Would you like a drink?" A woman appeared from behind Taryn startling her. Taryn was annoyed with her presence in the space. She rolled her eyes in disgust at the woman.

"No, thank you." Taryn didn't want anything to eat or drink. She didn't want to be there.

Ryan ordered a round of drinks for him and his friends as he picked up a pool stick and took the chalk and rubbed it against the end of the pool stick. "Let me get in the game. Who wants some of this?"

Taryn loved watching Ryan play pool, He was very competitive and always played to win. "Great shot, Babe." Taryn encouraged him throughout the game every time he made a shot.

"Thanks T." Ryan gave her a playful response.

The woman came back with the drinks and reminded Taryn that she was in a strip club. She was instantly annoyed again and even more angry at Ryan's response to the woman.

"Thanks sweetheart." Ryan looked at the woman like he wanted to eat her like a snack.

"Thanks for the drink, Bro." Ryan's friends all toasted as they took a sip of their drink. They continued playing pool and looking at the different women who would occasionally end up in the area where they were to see if they wanted a lap dance or private service.

Taryn felt so out of place and she didn't want to be there any longer. "Ryan, I'm ready to go. How many times have you had a lap dance or private services?"

"Don't start with me, Taryn. You wanted to come. So now you're here and now you're ready to go. Man, I can't win with you." Ryan was angry and it showed on his face.

"No! I didn't want to come here. I wanted to go to the movies. You wanted to come here and now I'm ready to go." Taryn clarified for Ryan why she was there.

"Okay, you know what. You're right. Let's go."

Ryan handed the pool stick to Ken. He gave him some money to pay for the drinks he had ordered.

"I'll be back, let me take her home."

"No, he will not be back."

Taryn angrily responded to Ryan's words to Ken.

Taryn headed for the door and she didn't wait for Ryan. He followed her and once they were both inside the car Taryn spoke.

"Do you want to be married?"

"What kinda question is that?"

"It's a serious one. This whole situation is a problem. It's a problem for our marriage. I've tried to deal with it, but I just can't."

"Taryn, what do you want me to do? I brought you so that you could see there was nothing going on and you're still not happy."

"No, I'm not happy. I don't want my husband in a place like that every Friday. I don't want to have to think about that. I don't understand why you got married if you still want to look at other women, especially naked women."

"I have told you it's not about the women. That's where we like to go to hang out. We play pool and have a few drinks and we go home."

"Yes! At two, three o'clock in the morning."

"Taryn, I'm grown. I can stay out and do what I want to do."

"You can't when you're married, Ryan. All that stuff is supposed to be done when you get married."

"Says who? I'm not doing anything I didn't do before we got married. Who told you I was going to change?"

"Okay! So, clearly, we don't see eye-to-eye on this. I'm tired and I'm done with this conversation…"

"Poor communication. Conflict. Lack of compromise. Broken trust. A definite recipe for disaster in a marriage." Socar had nailed it.

"For the rest of the ride home, I didn't say another word and neither did Ryan. Once we got home, Ryan pulled into the driveway and opened the garage. He opened the door to the house and let me in. I'll never forget how he made me feel and what he said…"

"I'll see you later. I'll be back." Ryan didn't even look at Taryn as he turned to leave.

"Why Ryan? Why is this so important to you? Why can't you stay home with me? Taryn grabbed his arm before he walked out the door.

"I've told you over and over this is not about you. Why do you have to make it about you? I'll see you later." He snatched his arm back and opened the door quickly closing it behind him…

"That door closing was symbolic if I can say so. He closed the door to his marriage and didn't even know it." Socar shook her head.

"Yep, he sure did. That moment was critical in the demise of our relationship. As I watched Ryan pull out of our driveway, it was clear to me our marriage was in trouble. Being his wife meant I had to accept the unacceptable. I no longer trusted Ryan, and the marriage was headed for destruction. It was just a matter of time."

CHAPTER 4

Becoming His Mother

"Learning to pray first before doing anything else is a skill, if mastered, has the greatest potential to transform any life." ~ Marcia E. Jackson

Socar realized it had gotten late. She and Taryn had been walking and talking for almost an hour.

"Baby-girl, I'm sorry to end our good time, but I have to get home. I have to prepare for church in the morning. Can we pick this up at a later time?"

Socar didn't wait for an answer. She walked in the direction of where her car was parked.

"Why don't you go. I can catch an Uber home."

"Are you sure?"

"Yes ma'am. Now that I'm out, I'm going to take advantage and enjoy this beautiful sunshine."

"I don't blame you. It is gorgeous down here near the water."

"Yes, it is! You know being near the water gives me life."

"I know! That's one of the reasons I chose to bring you down here."

"That's why I love you so. You always know what I need before I even know that I need it."

"God speaks. I just listen. You hear me?"

"Yes ma'am, I do. Who knows, I may even do a little shopping. You know a little retail therapy is always good for me."

"Yes indeed! A little RT never hurt nobody."

"Thank you again for everything today. You're the best!"

"Oh, you're welcome! It's always my pleasure. I'll call you later."

Taryn gave Socar a big hug and kiss on her cheek before she could turn and start walking to the parking garage.

Taryn found a wrought iron metal bench facing the Potomac River and she sat down quietly. After sitting for about fifteen minutes, her cell phone rang. She looked at the caller ID and it was her big sister, Yanna.

Taryn answered with a quiver in her voice.

"Hey sis, how are you?"

"Hey sis! I'm good! The question is, are you okay? You sound like something is wrong." Yanna and Taryn didn't talk every day, but from the time they were little, Yanna could always tell when something was bothering her little sister.

"Yeah, I will be okay. Socar just left. I was sharing some of my past experiences with her about Ryan. Took me back to a time that I've really tried to forget, and right now I'm feeling some kinda way about everything."

"Yeah, you wanna talk about it?"

"I don't know." Taryn's voice was shaking as she spoke.

"Where are you? I can hear noise in the background."

"I'm in Georgetown. I'm sitting here looking at the Potomac River. It's beautiful. Socar and I came down here to have brunch. I wasn't ready to leave, so I'm taking an Uber home later."

"Oh okay. Sounds like fun."

"Yep, it was fun," Taryn crossed her legs as she settled onto the bench.

"How is Socar?"

"She's great! Still doing all of what she does."

"Awesome! I'm in awe of her stamina and energy."

"It is quite impressive," Taryn moved her hair from her eye as the wind from the water continued to tussle her hair.

"So, what were you all talking about?"

"I was telling her about how Ryan and I met. And what happened with our marriage."

"You know, I never really knew what happened. You didn't share a whole lot. I figured you were probably embarrassed and trying to protect your feelings, so I didn't pry. But I've always wondered what happened to you guys. I can be a good listener if you need to talk through it more."

"Yeah, you know what…I really need to get this out." Taryn stood up and started walking along the pier. "Ryan and I used to come down here all the time when we were first dating. He would bring me down here on Friday nights when he was trying to hook me. Then he started hanging out with his so-called friends every Friday night and we couldn't make any plans on Friday."

"Every Friday night? Really!"

"Yes! One of the difficulties in our marriage was that Ryan would regularly go to a strip club on Friday nights. I let him know how much it bothered me, but he suggested that I come with him one time. Big mistake!

"I went with him. I was glad I did, but I vowed I would never go back. It wasn't a place for me. After I went, I really could not understand why Ryan continued to go. In my mind, I had envisioned something totally different from the reality. The truth was that many of the women were physically out of shape or just looked tired and worn out. The female dancers who were physically attractive seemed to be more interested in the other women who were surrounding the stage throwing dollar bills more than they were in the men who were trying to get their attention. The whole entire ordeal assured me that there was something very wrong with Ryan if he needed to be there instead of at home with me."

Taryn kept walking and continued talking. The sun was starting to set, and it was absolutely beautiful.

"The crazy thing was, I internalized all of it and it made me feel even more insecure and vulnerable. I concluded Ryan was cheating and there was nothing I could do about it. I felt stuck because I relied on Ryan to take care of me. I wasn't working at the time. We had agreed that I would be a stay-at-home mom to raise our kids. We were preparing to have a family. We were actually trying to get pregnant at the time. I didn't mind staying home, but I soon realized that this meant that Ryan was more dominant in our marriage. Sometimes I felt as if I didn't have a voice and it made me feel more like Ryan's property than his equal partner."

"Wow, I can't imagine you being such a strong woman trying to live like that. Mama didn't raise us to be that way." Yanna chimed in.

"Trust me, it was really hard. I realized I didn't know everything about Ryan's past life, and it was having a significant impact on his ability to keep up his end of the bargain to be the primary earner for our family. Being Ryan's wife meant doing things his way. It didn't matter if we were deciding financial matters, what furniture to buy or what to eat for dinner, Ryan's opinion would eventually win."

Taryn walked past some of the shops and stopped to look in the windows at the mannequin displays.

"It wasn't all Ryan's fault. I didn't always express my opinion because I didn't really care about the small details that Ryan seemed to pay too much attention to, but in the end, it mattered. I was somewhat passive when it came to managing my own life. It was easier for me to allow Ryan to take all the responsibility and I could just let him manage it all. I really sold myself short." Taryn owned her part in the failure of their marriage.

"How did you come out of it?" Yanna's voice piqued with curiosity.

"There just came a time where I grew spiritually and began to mature as a person. I began reflecting on what it meant for me to be Ryan's wife. I admitted that I had accepted some of his beliefs and his ideology and it did not always necessarily match my own values and how I was raised. I guess the saying 'to thine own self be true' comes to mind."

She stopped at a jewelry store window and admired the pieces showcased.

"There came a time in our relationship where I was no longer willing to try to fit into Ryan's way of doing life, and we began to spend less and less time together. The communication in our marriage was poor and neither of us knew how to fix it. I felt compelled to pay more attention to things that I had not questioned in the past and Ryan didn't seem to have answers for me that made sense."

"It's hard to save any relationship once the communication breaks down and the trust is broken. What kept you there? Because it sounds like this was before you all started a family?" Yanna sounded like she wanted to ask the question differently but couldn't figure out how.

"Shortly after all this, I found out I was pregnant. I dreamed of having a family with him. Before Ryan, I really hadn't thought about having children. When I dreamed about my future, my dream included the kind of career I would pursue, what kind of house I would live in, what kind of car I would drive and what different parts of the world I would travel to. I knew I would likely have a family one day, but that was not my primary concern. I felt I was too young to be worried about all that. Ryan changed my whole perspective on love, marriage and having a family." Taryn looked up, rolled her eyes and shook her head.

"Well, nobody could tell you anything once you met him. I remember how head over heels in love you were with him." Yanna and Taryn laughed.

"It wasn't all bad after we got married. I remember one moment in particular when we were working on getting pregnant and I was talking to Ryan…"

"I wonder what our children will look like?" Taryn and Ryan were lying next to one another and Taryn was staring out the frosted glass window of their cozy bedroom.

Ryan was halfway watching sports on television while halfway nuzzling up to Taryn.

"What do you want to name her if it's a girl?" Taryn asked

Ryan as she sat up in their king-sized bed stretching her arms high in the air.

"I don't know, Taryn, but let's work on making her right now." Ryan pulled Taryn back toward him and whispered in her ear as he gently kissed the back of her neck. The game wasn't as important to him any longer.

"TMI! Way too much information." Taryn and Yanna laughed hysterically.

"When we decided we would have a baby, we planned everything including making sure I was in my best health for the delivery of a healthy baby. I stopped using birth control and I began regularly working out. I ate more fruits and vegetables and I stopped drinking soda and alcohol altogether. I mostly drank water. I also started taking prenatal vitamins. I tracked the number of days of my menstrual cycle and when I realized after a few months that I had missed the first few days of my monthly cycle, I decided to take a pregnancy test. The test confirmed that I was pregnant. I was so excited to share the good news with Ryan. I called him at work…"

"Hey babe, what time are you coming home?" Taryn asked Ryan as she was planning a creative way to tell him that evening that he was going to be a father.

"I'm not sure. You know it's Friday, and the fellas and I are going to be hanging out." Ryan casually reminded Taryn.

"Yes, I know." Taryn was disappointed. She rolled her eyes folding her arms across her chest while juggling the phone on one shoulder.

She could feel her emotions starting to get the best of her and she decided to end the conversation with Ryan before the good news of their pregnancy was spoiled by a petty argument.

"Ok well, could you come home first? I need you to look at something for me before you go out with the fellas." Taryn quickly remembered why she had called him.

"Sure babe, I'll stop by the house as soon as I get off." Ryan responded.

"Ok, thanks babe. I'll see you later." Taryn clicked the off button on her phone.

She was excited that she had been able to convince Ryan to come home, and she was sure this would keep him in, at least for this evening. Ryan was relieved that Taryn had asked for what she wanted instead of just complaining about him going out every Friday. When Ryan arrived at home Taryn was waiting for him in their bedroom.

"Hey Taryn! Where are you?" Ryan yelled from the kitchen entrance that connected to the two-car garage.

"I'm in here!" Taryn yelled back.

Before entering the room. Ryan could smell strong scents of vanilla and lavender when he unlocked the door. Taryn had candles lit all around the room and she was wearing Ryan's favorite lingerie.

"Wow! I wasn't expecting this. What's going on Taryn?" Ryan slowly entered their bedroom without taking his eyes off her.

Taryn was leaning back on the bed as she extended her pointer finger and curled it toward her slowly, beckoning for Ryan to come over to her.

"Come over here. I have something for you." Taryn said in a flirtatious tone as she held out her hand that contained the positive pregnancy stick inside a slender box. The box was wrapped neatly in blue and pink stripped paper with a big blue and pink bow covering the entire top of the box.

"What is this, Taryn?" Ryan looked deeply into Taryn's eyes and she could see his excitement start to build as he was beginning to realize what she was trying to tell him.

"Oh my God, Taryn, are you saying...?" Ryan couldn't quite get it out as he was out of breath. He ripped the paper off the box and paused to gently open the top of the tiny box. He immediately saw what was inside and he jumped up off the bed grabbing the stick out of the box.

"Taryn, are we? Taryn, is this what I think it is?" Ryan was completely elated.

"Yes, it is Ryan. We are going to have a baby." Taryn smiled from ear to ear.

Ryan grabbed Taryn from the bed, kissed her deeply and he leaned down and touched her womb area.

"I can't believe this! I'm going to be a father." Ryan looked at the pregnancy stick again that was now laying on the nightstand.

"I can't wait to tell the fellas tonight. This is crazy!" Ryan let go of Taryn and walked toward the bathroom to freshen up for his evening out.

"Are you serious? You're still planning to go out tonight? After I just shared our good news? I was hoping we could celebrate." Taryn looked at Ryan. She was confused as her brow wrinkled. She shook her head back and forth.

"Taryn, please don't ruin this moment. You know this is my night with the fellas." Ryan responded to Taryn.

"Ryan, I just thought that you would want to share this moment with me. You can't miss one night with the fellas to spend it with me?" Taryn began to raise her voice.

"Taryn, please don't be like that. We will have our moment tomorrow night. I promise you. This is one of the best days of my life. Please just let me celebrate it with the boys tonight." Ryan pleaded.

"Just go, Ryan. Just go ahead and go." Taryn shook her head back and forth as she stared off into space while sitting on the edge of their bed.

"I promise we will do something fun tomorrow night to celebrate. I'll be back later." Ryan kissed Taryn on the forehead and headed toward the kitchen to the garage.

"I'm so sorry, sis. My God. I can't imagine what that must have felt like." Yanna's voice was shaking.

"I remember sitting for a long time before moving from that spot on the bed. A thousand thoughts rushed through my mind. I could not understand why Ryan was not able to settle into being the kind of husband I needed him to be." Taryn inhaled and exhaled deeply. "I wondered what kind of father he would be to our unborn child. I didn't know what to do next. I felt so lost. That was not what I envisioned for my life or my family. I was clueless about what to do to get Ryan to see what this was doing to our relationship." Taryn held her head in one hand.

"So, what did you do?" Yanna quietly asked.

"I said, Lord, I don't know what to do. I don't understand him, and I don't know if I can do this. Lord, please help me. I prayed and fell asleep with tears in my eyes."

CHAPTER **5**

Beloved Son

"Train up a child in the way he should go and when he is old he will not depart from it." Proverbs 22:6 (BSB)

Taryn decided it was finally time for her to get an Uber to take her home. Thankfully, her android phone would let her talk and schedule the Uber at the same time.

"What's that noise in the phone?" Yanna asked.

"Texting to order my Uber."

"Oh okay."

"Done!"

"Now, I gotta stay on the phone with you. You know some of these Uber drivers can be crazy." Yanna was protective of her little sister.

Taryn laughed, "Always being a big sis. I appreciate it though."

The Uber was there in minutes and Taryn climbed in and confirmed her address. The driver was a young African-American woman probably in her early twenties. Taryn continued talking to Yanna.

"Ryan was so attentive during the early stages of my pregnancy. Anything I wanted to eat; he made sure I had it. I will never forget the day when I was craving food from the Cheesecake Factory, one of my favorite restaurants at the time. We got all dressed up and went out to dinner. I ordered an appetizer and two entrees. I ate it all."

"Yes girl, pregnancy will make you eat like a pig." Taryn and Yanna laughed so hard until they both were in tears.

"Girl yes, these kids will make you eat everything in sight." She wiped tears from her eyes.

The Uber driver looked at Taryn through the rearview mirror. She was smiling.

Taryn spoke to her, "Please forgive me. My sister is a mess and she keeps me laughing."

The young woman spoke back to Taryn, "It's okay. I totally understand. When I talk to my sister, we do the same thing. You probably couldn't see it when you got in, but I'm pregnant. So, trust me, I understand."

Yanna heard her through the phone and the three of them laughed even harder.

"When is your baby due?" Taryn's joy for the driver came through in her voice.

"April."

"Is this your first one?"

"Yes ma'am."

"Congratulations! Motherhood is a beautiful thing."

"I believe you," she glanced again at Taryn.

Yanna chimed in, "Tell her it's gonna be okay."

Taryn put the phone on speaker so the driver could hear Yanna.

"Hi, my name is Yanna. What's your name?"

"It's Ada."

"Hi Ada! Nice to meet you. I told Taryn to tell you it's gonna be okay."

"Thank you, ma'am. I know it is. I used to worry about stuff. I know worry is not good for me or my baby. So, I just let it go now. God is in control."

"Exactly!" Yanna's voice echoed in the car.

"Have you had morning sickness since you've been pregnant?" Taryn questioned.

"Yes ma'am. It was so bad at one point, I had to take medication for it."

"Me too! I couldn't understand why they called it morning sickness. For me it was all day long sickness."

"Right!" Yanna was running water in the background.

"Mine has been mainly in the morning, but I'm past that now."

"Oh, I'm so glad for you. It can be miserable. I was just telling Yanna a story about when I was pregnant. You'll probably understand this. If you don't mind, I'd like to finish telling you both the story."

"I'm all ears," Ada touched her ear to confirm she was listening.

"Carry on, sis!" said Yanna through the speaker.

"With Ryan's food, Ryan is my ex-husband, the dinner totaled around a hundred dollars. Immediately after I finished all my food, I had to use the bathroom. Ryan began to worry because I was gone longer than usual. I still remember the conversation when I returned to the table…"

"Are you okay, Taryn?" Ryan looked concerned when Taryn returned to the table. She was sweating bullets and her lips were twisted. She didn't look well.

"No, I just got sick in the restroom. I threw up all my food. And now I'm hungry again." Taryn halfway chuckled through the terrible putrid taste left in her mouth.

"Already giving Mama trouble, huh?" Ryan raised his voice, as if the baby could hear him, and smiled as he looked at Taryn's stomach.

"Well, we can stop on the way home and get you something. What would you like?" Ryan shook his head and laughed.

"We could really go for a burger right now." Taryn rubbed her stomach as she stood up and put on her coat. Ryan assisted her.

"A burger it is. Let's go." Ryan had already paid the bill. On the way home they stopped at Burger King to get Taryn a Whopper with cheese, light mayonnaise, no tomato, cut in half with fries.

"That is a great story. I love it!" Yanna yawned.

Ada agreed with Yanna. "What was the most difficult part of your delivery? People keep telling me it's gonna be so hard."

"Other than being sick, I'm grateful I was able to carry to term and have a normal delivery. It was bad, but they have medication that can help. You'll be okay."

"Thank you for sharing that. Most people scare me with their stories."

"I think for me the most difficult thing was while I was celebrating becoming a mother, I was also grieving the loss of my grandma. Yanna, do you remember we lost Grandma Bella during my pregnancy?"

"Oh…you're so right! That was the same time. I forgot that. That was a really hard time for everyone. I remember feeling lost and empty during those first few days and months after she died. It was horrible." Yanna sounded more alert.

"Yeah…remember Grandma had been diagnosed with cancer by the time I was six weeks pregnant." Taryn sighed heavily. "Shortly after, she won her battle and earned her wings to transition home to be with the Lord. We were all devastated. Remember I didn't make it home in enough time to get to see her before she died." Taryn was misty eyed as that was still a sore spot for her.

"Oh my God! Yes…I remember. That must have made it even harder. I was so consumed with my own grief that I didn't have time to even think about what was going on with anybody else. I'm so sorry." Yanna apologetically confessed.

"No…we were all a mess and I totally understand. I had a really hard time with it and it affected my pregnancy. My doctor insisted I get a sonogram when I was about six weeks pregnant because I was having spotting. She thought I was having a miscarriage, and she told me that, which made everything worse. I was amazed the first time I heard my baby's little heartbeat echoing in that exam room at the hospital and seeing the tiny little image on the screen. It was amazing that life was growing inside of me. I was completely in awe of the miracle that Ryan and I had created."

"Aw! That is so sweet. I haven't had my first sonogram yet. I'm really excited to have it." Ada changed lanes to merge onto South Capitol Street from 395.

"Becoming a mother is such a beautiful experience. God is so amazing." Yanna exclaimed.

"Yes, and everything changed for me that Friday evening when my Damon was born. As predicted by my doctor for a first delivery, I had gone a day past my due date. I was exhausted. I was sleeping in a chair when my water broke in the early hours that Friday morning. Mom had come in town to be with me to help me and Ryan out with the new baby. We made our way to the hospital on that cold brisk morning in early March ready to meet the newest addition to our family. I labored all day with him and he finally entered the world just after six o'clock that evening. He was a surprise because Ryan and I had decided we didn't want to know the sex of the baby prior to his birth."

"Y'all were so good. There is no way I could've waited to find out." Yanna interrupted.

"Yeah! I don't think I will be able to wait. I wanna know right now." Taryn could see Ada's excitement as she looked at her face through the rearview mirror.

"Yeah, I get it! But we wanted to be surprised. When the doctor said it's a boy, both of us were overjoyed. We had predicted that it was a boy. Ryan was calling his friends and family and it wasn't long before they were all at the hospital to meet baby Damon and welcome him into the world. It was a beautiful Friday full of love and congratulations." Taryn shuffled her body on the back seat of the car and breathed out a deep sigh as she smiled looking out the window. I will forever treasure the beauty of that moment."

"So sorry I missed that day. I remember getting a call from Ryan right after Damon was born. He was so happy. You couldn't tell that man anything." Yanna smiled and shook her head.

"Then reality kicked in." Taryn was dry and blunt.

"What do you mean?" Yanna curiously asked.

"Even after I delivered Damon, Ryan left the hospital to go and be with his friends. It was Friday night." Taryn sarcastically reminded Yanna.

"Are you serious right now?" Yanna sucked her teeth.

Ada had a confused look on her face. Taryn continued.

"Yes! And I was too exhausted to even argue with Ryan about it. Mom was there so I really didn't care to focus on the fact that Ryan left me and our new baby that evening. I had my baby boy and he was healthy and absolutely gorgeous. I was so in love with Damon and completely enamored with what I had just experienced birthing him into the world. Honey, Ryan could've flown to the moon and I wouldn't have cared that night. Boy, bye!" They all laughed as Taryn held up two fingers.

"Girl, I hear you on that! I agree, I just had no idea all that was going on. Thank God you were stable and able to keep it all together. You are a soldier."

"Girl, I didn't do anything that many women before me haven't done. I had no choice but to fully embrace motherhood immediately." Taryn had never been responsible for anything so precious in her whole life. "And to think that God had entrusted me with a little life. I would be responsible for him as long as I was breathing." Like most moms, Taryn would seriously harm someone if she needed to keep Damon safe. In fact, she got very little rest in the hospital after Damon was born because she wanted to know where he was at all times.

"Ada, here's a piece of advice for you when you have your baby. Find some way to identify your baby. Find a unique mark or something that will let you know it's your baby."

"Okay, but it seems a little strange that I wouldn't know my baby." Ada's brow wrinkled.

"They practically all look alike when they're born…all red and wrinkly. Ryan and I talked about the hospital stay and how to make sure Damon wasn't one of those babies who got switched at birth or worse that he wasn't stolen from the hospital by someone desperate for a baby like one of those Lifetime movies."

"Are you serious?" Yanna and Ada laughed out loud.

"Yes, girl! I'm dead serious." Taryn laughed too.

"The minute he was born, I examined Damon and identified that he had a little birth mark on his hand that I used to make sure it was him while we were in the hospital. I wasn't playing at all. Every time they brought him to me, I would check his little hand." Taryn's voice got serious.

"Okay, thanks for the advice." Ada smiled.

Ada stopped the car in front of Taryn's house.

"Well Ada, it was so good to meet you. Best wishes for a healthy delivery. You're going to be a great mom. Trust yourself." Taryn searched her purse for her house keys.

"Thank you both. I really enjoyed our talk. Bye Yanna."

"Bye, so nice to talk to you, Ada. Take care."

Taryn got out of the car and stopped at the mailbox at the end of the driveway to collect her mail. She took the phone off speaker, put it up to her ear and held it with her shoulder while she opened the front door. She and Yanna continued talking.

"So how did things go once y'all left the hospital?" Yanna probed a little more.

"I completely acknowledge that I did not do a good job of balancing being a new mom with being a wife. Do you remember the time Damon and I came for a visit and I was complaining about Ryan? Remember what you told me..."

"Why doesn't he get it?" Taryn asked her sister, Yanna. "It's like I'm raising two children." Taryn sat down at the island in Yanna's kitchen.

"Taryn, you have to be patient with men. Some men just don't automatically know how to become a husband and a father. It's a big change for him too." Yanna was five years older than Taryn and she had learned a thing or two from making mistakes in her own marriage.

"I know. I'm just frustrated. I thought things would be different when we got married and we decided to have a child. I expected Ryan to grow up even though he said many, many times before that he had no intention of ever growing up." Taryn shrugged her shoulders, "I guess I should've listened."

"And what would you have done differently?" Yanna smiled at her sister. "You love Ryan. You two are just going through what a lot of couples go through when they get married and have children. It's a big change, just give it some time." Yanna grabbed Taryn's hand and held it while looking her in the eyes and encouraging her.

"Thank you, Sis. You always have the answers." Taryn hugged Yanna tightly praying she was right....

"Wow! Yes, I do remember that conversation. Clearly, I didn't know everything that was going on. I'm so sorry. My advice probably didn't help you."

"If only there had been an instruction manual to help me figure out how to be a wife and a new mom. I was totally smitten with Damon and I started to ignore Ryan. I can admit that today. We began growing more and more apart as I threw myself into motherhood. I wished that Ryan would've done the same, but he didn't share my feelings about it. He told me time and time again that he felt neglected after Damon was born. I thought it was immature and selfish of him because Damon was a baby and he needed me. I know now that my husband needed me too. I just didn't know how to do both."

"Taryn, many young women struggle in this area. Don't beat yourself up over it."

"He was really trying so hard too. Because of his support of our family, remember I was able to stay at home with Damon for the first two years of his life, which was a wonderful blessing. It allowed me to breastfeed Damon for his first year of life and we were attached at the hip. I was worried about Ryan as it seemed to be a lot of pressure on him and he seemed to pull away from me even more. I just didn't understand him anymore." Taryn was sitting in her window seat.

"I wish I had known. I wish I had been able to do more to help you both." Yanna struggled to get the words out.

"Ryan continued to live like he was a single man instead of a married man with a child. There were so many times when Taryn resented Ryan because he lived like he was single instead of the picture she'd painted for herself of a good husband and father. "I became judgmental of Ryan and it only added to the destruction of our family. I turned all my energy toward Damon and completely neglected Ryan, put Damon before Ryan in every way. This only made him even more insecure. He spent more time outside of our home. But that wasn't even the worst part."

"There's more?"

"There's a lot more." Taryn let out a big sigh.

"I can't believe this. Tell me."

Taryn's phone beeped. Taryn looked at it. It was Lisa.

"Lisa is calling me. We've been talking for a while. Let me take her call and we can talk later."

"Okay, no problem. I'm going to get ready for tomorrow. I have a long day. Love you."

"Thanks for listening sis. I love you too."

Taryn ended the call with Yanna and answered Lisa's call.

"Hey Lisa! Girl, how are you?"

"I'm good! How are you?" Lisa's voice raised an octave.

"I'm good too. Just been busy with work."

"Oh yeah, I totally understand that."

"These people want something from nothing, and they want it yesterday." Lisa sarcastically laughed.

"Tell me about it. I have a deal going on at work right now that has tested me in every way."

"Really! I'm surprised to hear that. You're usually so cool at work. What's up?

"Well, you know I shifted from residential to commercial real estate a while back."

"No, I don't' think I knew that. You're in with the Big Dawgs, huh? That's impressive."

"Exactly! It's a whole new world. I don't know how I feel about it. It's like I'm starting over after having built a solid professional reputation. I didn't expect this part of it."

"Yeah! But you've never been one to shy away from a challenge. I'm sure you will figure it out."

"Yeah, I'm sure I will. It's just my brokers expect me to close as quickly as I did before and it's taking longer. There are areas I'm not sure about and I don't feel like I can really go to them to ask for support. They say I can get support, but what that looks like is them giving the deal to someone else to close."

"Yeah, when there is a lot of money on the table, companies aren't usually very supportive. They just want to make sure their interests are protected."

"Exactly! That's why I love talking to you because you get me."

"Yep, we've been friends too long for me not to get you, and unfortunately I've been there and done that."

"You know as I think of it, the couple I'm working on this deal with, Mr. and Mrs. Abdullah, remind me of me and Ryan back in the day."

"Seriously, how so?" Lisa chuckled.

"They're young and ambitious. I love that about them. They own many residential properties and are now working on acquiring commercial properties."

"Oh yeah! You and Ryan were investing in real estate when y'all were together. I think I forgot that. Whatever happened with that?" Lisa asked genuinely curious as Taryn had not talked about it much.

"Funny, I just hung up with Yanna. I've been talking to her for hours about the past with me and Ryan."

"Really, what were y'all talking about?"

"We took a trip down memory lane."

"Oh really! Well let's go. Don't leave me out of the loop."

"Okay, if you insist."

"Yes ma'am, I insist. Spill the beans Roomie."

"Well, it all started with Socar this morning. She stopped by and I was telling her the story of how we met John and Ryan over brunch. Remember that?" Taryn hugged her knees.

"Girl, how could I ever forget? Those were some of the best days of our lives." Lisa chuckled.

"Yeah! Our crazy college days." Taryn laughed too.

"Yes, things were definitely simpler back then."

"Yep! No responsibility…just go to school and party."

"Wait! I thought you said you were talking to Yanna?"

"I was, she called after Socar and I ended our brunch. I was telling Yanna about my pregnancy with Damon. I realize I never really told anyone how bad things got between me and Ryan. I was embarrassed and ashamed."

"I'm pretty sure I don't know about anything you would have to be embarrassed or ashamed about. What happened?"

"Are you sure you want to hear all of this?"

"First of all, I'm mad you never talked to me about it while you were going through. But I understand how it can be sometimes, especially since I've been married to John for so long. Hit me with it."

"Okay! Let me take you back to a day that I will never forget. That day changed my life and my marriage forever…"

CHAPTER **6**

Beyond the Secrets

"Whoever dwells in the shelter of the Most High will rest in the shadow of the Almighty." Psalm 91:1 (NIV)

"When I was six months pregnant with Damon, I learned that Ryan was gambling heavily, and things had gotten out of control. On more than one occasion, his habit had left us in the red financially. We began arguing about money. There was one argument in particular..."

"Ryan, I need money to buy groceries. What account should I use?" Taryn asked Ryan one Saturday afternoon.

"Can't you just use one of the credit cards? Ryan responded as he was still lying in bed at three o'clock in the afternoon.

"To buy groceries? Why would I need to buy groceries with a credit card? That doesn't make sense." Taryn fired back at Ryan shaking her head back and forth, peering at him as her forehead wrinkled in concern.

"Taryn, please don't start with me. Just do what I told you to do..."

"I remember he raised his voice and sat up on the bed. He acted like he was talking to a child. I stopped in the middle of the room, jerked my head back and tilted it to the side as I stared at him for a full ten seconds. I asked myself, *Who on Earth does he think he's talking to?*" Taryn blinked her eyelashes as if she was trying to get something out of her eye.

"I've seen that look before and I know it very well." Lisa laughed.

"Yes, you do. He sent a look back across the room at me that let me know if looks could kill, I would've been dead at that moment. I sensed this was not the time to challenge Ryan, but I made a mental note that I didn't like the way he spoke to me. I also didn't trust him. We had established a level of transparency around our finances even though Ryan controlled them. I knew in that moment that something was very wrong. I believed whatever he was doing was happening during his little Friday night excursions. He was spending every Friday night outside of our house going to the strip club and doing whatever else he thought he was big and bad enough to do."

"Every Friday night? Wow, what married man does that?"

"Exactly! I was so tired of Ryan running out of the house every Friday night, that I decided I was going to find out exactly what was going on with him."

"And you had every right to know what was going on. You were his wife."

"Absolutely! I knew it was more than just hanging out at a strip club playing pool every Friday night with his so-called friends. So…here it was another Friday night at two o'clock in the morning and Ryan still wasn't home. I went through my usual routine of calling him back-to-back for about thirty to forty-five minutes with no answer. I was hormonal from the pregnancy and I felt his disrespect of me and our marriage needed to be addressed, in the moment, around the people he was so loyal to. I was fired up and ret to go…literally."

"Yeah…and what happened?" Lisa was on edge…

"I got up out of bed, struggling as I searched for clothes to wear. Everything I owned was too small, and whatever I was about to confront with Ryan, I didn't want to look too crazy doing it. I knew it was already crazy that a woman who was six months pregnant would be out in the streets at that hour of the morning searching for her husband. However, I was at a point where I could no longer turn my head the other way and ignore the warning signs that my marriage and family were in trouble. I had been pretty passive up until this point and I was just simply tired. The memory of it all is still so fresh for me…"

"I'm so sick of this! Why did he even get married if all he wants to do is hang out? We have this baby on the way, and he hasn't slowed down yet. What am I supposed to do with all this? This is not what I wanted when I said, 'I do'." Taryn was filled with anger and resentment as she paced the floor back and forth talking out loud to herself.

She moved to the bathroom to wash her face and brush her teeth and her hair. "I can't tell anyone about this. People will judge me and think that I should leave Ryan. They don't like him anyway." She flung the toothbrush back in the holder. "I know he can be a lot, but when he's not taken over by whatever is going on with him, he's really a great guy. If only people could see this." She found one of Ryan's baseball caps and put it on. She adjusted the back so it fit snugly on her head.

Taryn reached into the closet and grabbed her favorite pair of Ugg boots. She slipped them on with no socks. She grabbed her wool coat, warm gloves lined with wool, and tied her wool scarf around her neck before heading out the door to get into her car. "I can't call my girlfriends; they just won't understand. I can't call my mother. She will definitely tell me to leave him. My dad will probably fly up here and get me. My brother will want to kill him. Lord, what am I going to do?" She rested her head on the steering wheel. "Please help me get through this Lord." Taryn was willing to fight for her marriage, but she needed to know what was going on to know how to fight.

"Yep, that was a completely crazy time, and I did what I had to do. We owned a second property that was a six-unit apartment building in the city. We were renovating it with hopes of renting it out for residual income. We had one tenant who lived there, and he was Ryan's friend. The thought that Ryan might be there entered my mind. It was a windy, cold December night. There was little traffic on the road. I passed a car here and there along my drive. It had snowed a few days before and there were dirty piles of snow on the side of the road. I wondered if it was safe for me to be out as there might have been ice patches on the road, so I drove carefully."

"Why on Earth would you be out there at that time of night?" Lisa grew more and more angry as Taryn continued the story.

Completely dismissing Lisa's question, Taryn continued. "I pulled up and saw Ryan's car parked on the street in front. The street parking in front of the building was all taken, and I had to park on the opposite side of the street and cross over. It was usually a very busy street and crossing it would have been difficult any other time. Thankfully, there were no cars driving up and down the street due to the early morning hour."

"Girl, you must have been furious." Lisa sat down on her couch and crossed her legs.

"I was! Immediately, I felt the anger and rage causing my stomach to twist in knots. The baby inside my womb had been sleeping the whole time, but he seemed to know that I was in distress which made him start moving around. I remember touching my stomach out of concern for my unborn child as my motherly instinct knew this was not a good internal environment for my baby. This made me even more angry and resentful toward Ryan since it was his fault that I was out at that hour searching for him. I sat in the car talking to myself…"

"Lord, what am I going to find when I go in this place? Give me strength right now, Father." Taryn prayed knowing this moment would likely change her life.

"Girl…this is too much. Wait a minute. So, you're sitting in front of the building and you see his car? I can't." Lisa was totally enthralled.

"Yes! I wanted to storm inside yelling, cursing and screaming at Ryan and whoever was in there with him. I also thought deeply about what this moment would mean for our marriage. I sat in the car for at least fifteen minutes contemplating what I would find inside once I opened that door. I had to decide if I was truly ready to confront Ryan. At that moment, I held my head because I was battling a thousand thoughts flooding my mind. I wanted to drive back home and wait for Ryan to come home later that morning. I knew if I did that, I wouldn't be true to myself. I was tired of lying to myself that it was okay for Ryan to continually disrespect me. I was tired of wondering what was going on. I was tired of acting like everything was okay. I was just tired, and I needed to know what was going on to be able to deal with it. It was the wondering that was driving me crazy. I decided I was going in. I vividly remember everything that happened after that..."

Taryn unlatched her seatbelt and opened the car door. She climbed out of the car and stood looking at the building. The entrance to the building was fully lit and there were lights on inside both the downstairs apartments. She crossed the street and walked up to the door of the building and paused for a moment to listen. There seemed to be a party going on inside. Taryn could hear music, loud voices and laughter coming from inside. She stood there for a moment listening to see if she could hear Ryan's voice. She heard Ryan laughing and once she heard his voice, her anger raged as she stuck her key in the door to open the lock. She turned the knob and stepped inside ready to crack his skull.

The entrance to the building smelled like cigarette and marijuana smoke. There was go-go music playing, and the door to the first-floor apartment to the left of Taryn was open. There were people standing near the entrance and others inside the open door to the apartment. She didn't recognize any of the people, and she thought they must have been friends of the tenant who lived there, even though his apartment was upstairs on the second floor. It had been a while since she had been over to the apartment complex and she wasn't even aware that the downstairs apartment had been completely renovated. She wondered why Ryan had not told her about it and better yet, why it had not been rented to a tenant for income.

"Excuse me!" Taryn pushed past a man and a woman standing near the entrance of the apartment. The woman looked very familiar. Taryn remembered her from the strip club the one time she went with Ryan.

"What are you doing here?" Taryn rolled her eyes at her and spoke through clenched teeth as she passed her.

The woman immediately knew who Taryn was, and she whispered to the guy she was talking to as she nodded her head in Taryn's direction.

"That's Ryan's wife. Time to go!" She whispered, but Taryn heard her. Since being pregnant, her hearing had heightened. They immediately shuffled out of the apartment into the foyer area and scurried out the front door.

Taryn heard the door slam behind them. She quickly focused her attention back on the mission, which was to find Ryan. Apparently, he had been quite busy fixing up this apartment. In the middle of the floor was a huge pool table. There were at least eight men and women standing around the pool table watching as two men were engaged in a game. Taryn didn't stop to count the people in the room, and the men playing pool were focused on making their shots. The others standing around were making bets about who would win the game and exchanging money. Taryn didn't recognize any of the people. She kept walking into the next room, which was the dining room. There was a card table set up and four people sitting around the table playing what looked like poker. Taryn wasn't sure because she didn't know how to play poker. They were engrossed in their game and didn't notice as she passed them.

Taryn could now hear Ryan's voice clearly, so she was getting closer to him. On the right side of the room was a bar set up and there was a man serving drinks. He looked at Taryn like she was a pregnant lady in the wrong place at the wrong time and asked if he could help her.

"Yes, you can. Where's Ryan?" Taryn smiled at the man with a he's-in-big-trouble smile, which caused his raised eyebrow.

With a concerned look on his face, the man pointed to the next room toward the kitchen. Taryn headed in that direction as she noticed another table set up in the corner of the room with more people playing cards and making bets.

"Ryan, what on earth is going on here?" Taryn screamed as she entered the back room where Ryan was sitting at a table with three other men sitting around it, each holding a hand of cards. There were also two women standing near Ryan who backed away once they realized who Taryn was.

"Babe, what are you doing here?"

Ryan stood up from the table with a confused look on his face. He walked toward Taryn and took her by the arm leading her back to the front of the apartment. There was so much going on that the people didn't even notice them.

"Why didn't you call me?" Ryan said as he pulled his phone from his pocket.

"I've been calling you all night. What is going on in here?" Taryn snatched her arm away after they stopped near the front door.

"It's just a little card game. Me and some of the fellas get together and we play cards, Baby. It's nothing, just me and the fellas hanging out having a good time." Ryan tried to explain, but Taryn wasn't buying it.

"Ryan, I don't know what is going on with you. I don't know what is going on in here."

"You don't need to know. It doesn't concern you. It's nothing you should be worried about."

"What do you mean I don't need to know? It does concern me. If it concerns you, it concerns me. We're married, remember! Who are these people? Is this why we don't have any money?"

"They're my friends. People I know from work. People I grew up with. You don't know everyone that I know. And we do have money."

"Why have I never met them? And who are these women you have in here all over you.?"

"There you go again with that jealousy crap. I'm not doing anything with any other woman."

"Then why are they hanging all over you? Why are you here?"

"Taryn, I've told you time and time again. Fridays are my time. My time to chill with my friends. To do what I want to do for me with my time."

"That's not what you do in a marriage, Ryan."

"Says who? Who made that rule in our marriage?"

"I did. I expect you to act like a married man."

Taryn and Ryan were on two different pages. They each had an idea of what marriage should be, but their ideas were no match for their reality. As the crowd began to watch the interaction between Ryan and Taryn, Ryan became bolder in front of his so-called friends.

"And what does a married man look like to you? Where did your idea of what a married man looks like come from?"

"Partnership in every way. Marriage is partnership. Not one person doing whatever they want to do whenever they want to, at the expense of the other person and the marriage."

"We are partners, Taryn. I didn't sign up for marriage to completely lose myself and neither did you."

"No one is asking you to lose yourself, but this is crazy. Look around at all this that I didn't even know was going on. Why didn't you tell me about any of this? This doesn't feel like a partnership Ryan."

"There's no reason for me to tell you anything. There's nothing that concerns you here to tell."

"Okay, and I can tell you really believe that Ryan. I mean, I'm not sure I even know you anymore. I call you all night, you don't answer. You've got me out here on the road at all times of night worried about you. I can't do this. You need to shut this down and come home now."

Taryn insisted as Ryan tried to quiet her as people continued watching them. The music had stopped playing for a few minutes.

"Babe, I can't just shut this down and come home. I want you to go home and I'll be there in a few. We can talk when I get there."

Ryan moved Taryn out of the apartment where everyone was into the empty apartment across the hall and closed the door for privacy.

"Ryan, why can't you shut it down? What is this?" Taryn's voice began to tremor, and she was shaking.

"Babe, I'll explain it all when I get home. Go home and rest and we will talk about it. I promise." Ryan assured her.

"Stop calling me Babe! Ryan, you need to come home now. This is crazy! What have you gotten yourself into here?" Taryn demanded as she paced back and forth in the empty, dimly lit room.

"Listen to me, I will be home when I finish. You need to go home, and we will talk about it when I get there." He raised his voice at her and pointed toward the door.

Taryn shook her head, threw up both her hands and surrendered as she walked toward the door "Okay Ryan, you win. I can't..."

"I don't even know what to say. I'm completely speechless right now. If I didn't know you, I would swear this story is made up." Lisa was dumbfounded.

"I know...it's crazy...right? I looked back at Ryan with tears in my eyes as I closed that front door behind me. The winter cold immediately slapped me in my face and I wrapped my open coat around me and tied a knot. As I walked toward the car, I could only feel an overwhelming numbness throughout my entire body. I knew my husband was in trouble and there was nothing I could do to help him. I drove back home in complete silence thinking of how I could save myself and my unborn child."

Taryn shivered as she recalled that unsavory day in her life. Ryan had been living a secret life she had no clue about until she entered the apartment that fateful night. Her instincts had been right. Something about that Friday night felt different for her, and had she not gone to the apartment that night, she would have never known what Ryan was into.

"I absolutely cannot believe you went through all of this and you didn't say anything," Lisa was dumbfounded.

"I didn't know what to say. I was so lost and confused, broken and ashamed."

"And you still stayed with him after that night?" Lisa was struck by what she had heard.

"Yes, I did."

"And gave birth to a healthy baby boy."

"Yes, thank God!"

"And tried to make it work."

"Yep, after all that."

"Why? How?"

"Because that's what we do as women, even at the expense of our well-being and sanity."

"Ain't that the truth."

"You know Ryan said something important that night that I'm just now getting."

"What was that?" Lisa's curiosity overtook her.

"That we should never lose ourselves in marriage. He was right." Taryn played with a loose thread on her top.

"I don't know about that," Lisa mumbled.

"No, his method was madness, but he was right about keeping something for yourself, even in marriage."

"I'm curious about how you managed after that night. Because from the outside looking in, I wouldn't have ever known anything like this was happening in your life."

"It wasn't easy, but by the grace of God I made it. A lot happened after that night.

"Please tell me. I can't believe you kept all of this to yourself."

"Okay, if you have the time, I'm happy to share more. Let me pour myself a glass of wine. I need to mellow out for this."

Taryn took a sip of wine after she settled into the couch to finish telling Lisa about her experience.

CHAPTER 7

Falling Apart

"Be careful thinking you know what it took for someone to have the life they have or the relationship they have, because you may not be able to withstand the troubles they have." ~ Marcia E. Jackson

"Talking about this is really helping me work through some things. I'm so glad you called, Lisa, and that you are willing to listen." Taryn had been friends with Lisa since childhood. Their bond was unbreakable. Taryn didn't want to bother Lisa while she was going through her marital woes, especially since Lisa's husband, John, was one of Ryan's closest friends.

"It's helping me too. Besides listening to this story, there ain't nothing else better going on for me right now. This is making me think about some things in my own life. Keep going."

"Okay. Once I knew Ryan was gambling, he didn't hide it anymore. You know…now that I think about it…we really never talked about that night when I caught him gambling. He came home and here's what happened…"

Taryn was still in bed when Ryan eventually came home around ten o'clock that Saturday morning. She hadn't slept soundly at any point throughout that early morning and she was completely exhausted mentally and physically. She didn't feel like talking to him. She didn't even want to see him she was so disgusted.

She had been thinking about everything since she arrived back home. It was clear to her that she didn't know her husband anymore. She no longer trusted him, and she definitely didn't respect him. She no longer loved him like she used to. The lies and deceitfulness made her resent him. They made her question everything about the relationship and their marriage. Taryn was angry with him, but she was mostly angry with herself for being so naïve. She was flabbergasted that she didn't know about the building renovations and the gambling that was taking place there. She couldn't understand why Ryan would jeopardize everything that they had worked so hard to build. Especially for people that she didn't even know.

"Who are these people, and why is he so invested in all this? Why would he be willing to lose his family?" Taryn repeated these questions to herself over and over again.

She had so many questions she wanted to ask Ryan, but she was just too exhausted. She heard him come in the house and fumble around for a while before climbing into bed next to her without speaking a word. Taryn could smell the stench of smoke and liquor mixed with a vague scent of her favorite cologne. It filled the entire room, and it smelled disgusting.

"He didn't even think to shower before getting in this bed. So disrespectful!" Taryn whispered so softly. She was pissed.

Taryn didn't move even though she wanted to immediately get out of the bed. Her back was toward Ryan, so she prayed hard that he wouldn't know she was awake. She decided she would wait until he fell asleep and then get up. A few minutes passed and Ryan was snoring like a drunk. She couldn't stand the sight of him, nor did she want to hear his liquor-induced snoring. Ryan always snored louder when he drank. Taryn slowly got up and moved to the guest bedroom so she could be overtaken by sleep.

After that, every time Taryn tried to talk to Ryan about his gambling, he would come up with an excuse not to address it.

"Ryan, we need to talk about the other night." Taryn looked across the kitchen at Ryan who was lying on one end of the sectional sofa in the living room watching a football game.

"Do we really have to do this right now Taryn, really?" Ryan responded without taking his eyes off the game.

"Yes, we do!" Taryn demanded.

Ryan looked over his shoulder from the couch. "Well, I don't want to right now. Look, you need to just let it go. I've told you it's just me and the fellas playing cards. No big deal."

"He tried to make it seem as if I was crazy and he wasn't really involved in gambling. Our bank accounts told a different story. We were in debt and it had gotten so bad that we were using credit cards to purchase food and household items. That would soon run out and I knew it was only a matter of time. Ryan continued to go out on Friday nights, and he even began gambling through the week. On the outside, everything looked fine because I still held everything together for a while. But things were quickly falling apart. From day to day, Ryan was either late for work or he wasn't going to work at all. He eventually lost his job. Thankfully, a few years after Damon was born, I was able to find work. This only made Ryan angry because now I was earning the money in the house and I had to completely separate my financial life from his. He wasn't earning any money and once the credit cards ran out, he became angry when I wouldn't give him money." Taryn grew sad as she recounted this tragic time in her life.

"I can only imagine." Lisa didn't know what to say.

"The gambling consumed him. There was no reasoning with him. Ryan was unwilling to get treatment and I couldn't deal with it all. The shame I felt about not knowing how to navigate the addiction was the worst part. When I did develop the nerve to share it with a few people, it was clear to me that they did not seem to know what to do or how to help. It made me sorry that I even took the step to reach out to others. It was hell for me watching Ryan destroy his life and our family. I continued to watch as our world was shattering right before my eyes." Taryn poured her heart out to Lisa.

"It only got worse after Damon was born. I felt like a married single mother. I was raising Damon by myself. Ryan was inconsistent and unavailable to assist in Damon's care or provide financial support. He didn't help me with childcare expenses, or any other expenses related to Damon."

"That had to be hard. Daycare is no joke." Lisa could relate to the reality of daycare costs.

"Yeah…it was. I struggled for about three years before I decided it was time to end the marriage. It was over long before then, I just needed the time to help me come to terms with it," Taryn recounted for Lisa. "Man, those were some really hard times back then. I had to move me and Damon out of our home because it was going into foreclosure. Ryan forced me to leave. We had already lost the apartment building. That was the time I almost moved back home."

"I wish you had. At least you would've been closer to family." Lisa shared.

"Well, I'm glad I didn't." Taryn chimed back with a slight laugh. "Thankfully, I was able to find a two-bedroom apartment for me and Damon to move into on the other side of town away from Ryan. Financially, I was struggling to take care of myself and Damon based on my salary alone. At the same time, I found peace in my own space. I didn't have to argue with anyone or wonder when or if he was coming home or if he was hurt or dead somewhere. As hard as it was to leave and live on my own as a single mom, it was also completely liberating." Taryn looked for the bright spot in her situation.

"Absolutely! Having your own space away from the craziness I'm sure made a big difference…gave you a different perspective of what could be." Lisa agreed.

"Yup! That's exactly what happened. I was able to stand on my own two feet. I had to figure things out and make it work… and I did." Taryn looked around at her current surroundings.

"But what helped you to move on and actually go through with the divorce? Lisa wanted more of the details.

"Well, that was pretty clear one day when Ryan showed up at my house with his girlfriend to pick up Damon for a visit." Taryn let the cat out of the bag.

"What? Girl, you better stop lying. I know that…didn't." Lisa started to say a curse word but stopped herself to remain respectful of Taryn's feelings.

"Girl, yes he did. I knew I had to file, but in order for me to file for divorce, I had to be physically separated from Ryan a year. It had already been six months and I was anxiously waiting for the next six months to pass. I still loved Ryan, but

I could not deal with the lifestyle he had chosen for himself. I was unwilling to compromise on that. Besides, Ryan had seemingly already moved on."

Taryn peered out the window one day when Ryan pulled up to pick up Damon for a visit. He was driving a car that Taryn didn't recognize. There was a woman in the car with him. Taryn was shocked that Ryan would be so bold to bring a woman to her home. But she had already figured Ryan was dating someone. He wasn't the type of man to be alone for any period of time let alone six whole months.

"The car he's driving must be hers." Taryn huffed. "The nerve of him to show up here with a woman. How dare he?" Taryn whispered to herself, slowly shaking her head back and forth, as she separated the mini blinds to try to get a better look at them.

"Damon, your dad is here." Taryn yelled to her son who was in his room in the back of the two-bedroom apartment.

Taryn opened the front door of the apartment. Damon came running down the hallway with his little backpack filled with clothes and his favorite toys on his back.

"Ryan, who is that?" Taryn ripped into Ryan as soon as she opened the door. "Why would you bring some woman over here? And why would you have her around my son?" She was hurt.

"Well, hello to you to, honey!" Ryan responded mockingly with a smug grin on his face.

"Daddy! Daddy! Daddy!" Damon yelled as he pushed past Taryn to jump up into Ryan's arms.

"Hey lil man. How are you?" Ryan hugged Damon tightly. "Man, you're getting so big. What have you been eating?" Ryan and Damon both laughed heartily as they turned to leave.

Taryn stopped them, "When are you bringing him back?" Taryn knew the answer, she just wanted him to confirm it.

"On Sunday." Ryan responded looking back at Taryn. They had already talked about it, so he figured she was just being childish.

"Okay. Come here and give Mommy a kiss, Damon." Taryn reached her arms out for Damon.

"Bye Mommy!" Damon reached over from Ryan's arms and hugged Taryn goodbye.

"Be good, baby. I love you." She kissed Damon's cheek and stood back as Ryan opened the door to leave.

"Truth be told, I was glad to have a weekend to myself, but I was definitely going to miss Damon for the few days that he was spending with Ryan. I couldn't stop wondering who the woman was with Ryan. Damon was almost four so he could let me know if anyone was mistreating him. Even though Ryan had his flaws, I knew he would never let anything happen to our son. Since he had obviously moved on, I planned to take the weekend to hang out with friends and do something fun and different. Maybe I would meet someone and go on a date."

"He ain't the only one who can get someone else. I'm going out this weekend with my girl, and I'm gonna have a great time. Let me call Dreya to see what's going on this weekend." Taryn picked up the phone and dialed Dreya's number.

Taryn had met Dreya at work and they instantly became friends. They would go to lunch every day and talk about work and life. Dreya enjoyed Taryn's company and invited her to attend a few parties. Taryn had not taken her up on the invite because she just wasn't in the mood to find a babysitter for Damon nor did she have any extra money to spend going out.

It was also just too much trouble for the mental space Taryn was in during those earlier times when Dreya invited her out.

Dreya had modeled and acted in a few commercials, and she had a small part in at least one movie. As a result, she knew some people in the entertainment industry. She had good connections and used her social capital to keep a full party calendar. She usually got invited to all the big parties in cities across the country and the world. If there was anyone who knew what was going on around town, it was Dreya. Dreya was a few years older than Taryn. She was a long five feet eleven inches without heels with a medium complexion and a small frame. Her beautiful, long curly black hair was always straightened because she hated her curls, even though most women would have loved to have them. Without even trying, her presence automatically filled every space of any room.

"Hey girl! How are you?" Dreya was always so cheerful when she answered the phone.

"I'm good. I'm calling because I have a free weekend. I know I've missed several invites to hang out with you, but I'm ready this weekend. Damon is with his dad and I'm trying to figure out what to do with myself. What's going on this weekend?"

"Oh girl, that's awesome! You know there's always a party or two happening. I was invited to two parties tomorrow night. You wanna come with me?" Dreya's voice went up an octave.

"Yes, count me in." Taryn snapped her fingers three times in the air.

Dreya provided the details, and Taryn was even more excited. She began thinking about what she would wear. It had been such a long time since she had been out with a friend to have a good time. Working and raising Damon had been her single focus. It would be nice to get away and be around new people. Dreya offered to pick her up for the party. Taryn had shared some of the details with Dreya about her failing marriage and she was supportive of Taryn moving on. They ended the call and agreed to meet the next evening.

Dreya arrived on time to pick Taryn up for the party. "You look so pretty. You might meet one of these eligible bachelors tonight. You know, someone nice. There are going to be a lot of professional men at the party." Dreya teased Taryn when she got in the car. They both laughed.

Taryn sucked her teeth. "Girl, I don't want to meet anyone. I just want to hang out, have a good time and come on back home. Besides, I'm still married...for now." Taryn held up her ring hand and pointed to her empty ring finger where her wedding ring used to be.

"Ok, I understand. No pressure." Dreya threw up her hands.

They finally arrived at the party and pulled up to a beautiful mansion. The eggshell white colonial style home was flanked by two large pillars set back off the street on a long winding driveway. The yard had been professionally landscaped and each blade of grass looked as if it had been cut with scissors. There were at least three well-lit entrances in the front of the house and several rows of steps leading up to each entrance. Lights adorned the driveway on both sides and two very expensive vehicles were waiting in front of them to be valet parked.

"Wow, this is nice!" Taryn exclaimed. It was their turn to park the car. Two of the eight young valet guys opened their car doors and extended their hands to help both Taryn and Dreya out of the car.

"Welcome ladies." The two handsome young guys said almost simultaneously.

Dreya led the way, and Taryn followed her up the middle entrance to the home. Before they could knock or ring the doorbell, a tall man dressed in a black tuxedo opened the door for them and welcomed them into the home. Once inside, Dreya was greeted by several people she knew. She immediately introduced Taryn and made her feel comfortable being there. Dreya found the couple who was throwing the party and introduced Taryn to them as well. The woman invited Dreya to follow her into her office to discuss a potential business opportunity, which would leave Taryn alone for a few minutes.

"Hey, I'll be right back. You okay?" Dreya looked at Taryn with raised eyebrows.

"Absolutely! Take your time." Taryn was so happy to be out she didn't mind Dreya leaving her for a while.

"I could get used to this." Taryn looked around and moved through several rooms where people were having conversations and dancing to the music that was playing.

The food was good. There were plenty of drinks and beautiful people who seemed to all be happy and having a good time. It was a great party with amazing ambience. It made Taryn forget about her real life for a minute. It felt good to be out of the house for a change.

"Excuse me. I couldn't help but notice how beautiful you are." A man said as he approached Taryn from across the room. "Are you here alone?"

"No, I came with a friend." Taryn blushed looking away from him to scan the room for Dreya.

Taryn had noticed him staring at her when they first came in. He had waited patiently for his moment to approach her. He looked to be everything a woman would want in a man. He was tall - about six feet three inches - dark and handsome with broad shoulders, a chest and arms that bulged through his shirt. Taryn became uncomfortable because she could see herself getting a big bear hug and having those big muscular arms wrapped around her. It had been more than fourteen years since Taryn had even talked with another man let alone seen herself making love to one.

"What's your name?" His voice oozed with sexiness.

"Wow, he's fine." Taryn slowly mumbled to herself before responding with her name. "It's Taryn." She looked him in the eyes as he extended his hand to shake hers.

"Taryn." He licked his lips as her name exited his mouth. That's a beautiful name for a beautiful woman." He held on to her hand and kissed it. "Taryn, I'm Michael." He was still holding on to Taryn's hand.

"It's good to meet you, Michael." Taryn said in her Southern Belle way as she gently and playfully pulled her hand away from him.

The energy between the two of them was automatic and intense. Taryn was definitely out of her comfort zone. Yet, she was enjoying the attention and the connection. Taryn could be flirtatious, and she remembered in that moment that she had enjoyed flirting in the past. The two had several exchanges but could barely hear one another over the music. They decided to move to the outside patio to hear one another better.

"So, Taryn, tell me a little bit about yourself." Michael placed his hand on her back as they moved to an outside patio that was less noisy and more intimate.

"What do you want to know?" Taryn was guarded, yet she continued to politely smile.

"Who is Taryn? That is the million-dollar question." Michael moved in closer and looked intensely into Taryn's eyes. He was in her personal space, and she could smell his musk scented cologne. He had beautiful white teeth and a killer smile with deep long dimples on both cheeks and a cleft chin that Taryn was convinced she could stare at all day and night.

"I'd rather hear more about you." Taryn redirected as she wasn't ready to share.

"Well, I'm single. I've never been married. I have two kids. I own my own business." Michael was much more open to sharing.

"Okay." Taryn smiled. "Single, never been married, two kids, own business." She repeated it to make sure she got it correct.

"That's right. What about you, Taryn?" Michael questioned again.

Taryn didn't want to tell him that she was still married but separated. She didn't know if that would end their conversation. She didn't want it to end just yet. She was intrigued by Michael.

"It's complicated." Taryn playfully touched Michael's rock-hard chest with her pointer finger.

"Well, we have the night. Why don't you break it down for a brother?" Michael laughed.

Taryn let down her wall and explained to Michael that she and Ryan were separated, and that divorce was impending.

She told him about Damon and about her work. She didn't get into the details of why she and Ryan were divorcing, but said they mutually agreed it was best for them to go their separate ways. Michael didn't seem to be moved by Taryn's story. He empathized with her situation and shared a bit about his past relationship that didn't work out. Michael did ask a question that made Taryn sad about how things between her and Ryan had turned out.

"Just curious, Taryn, when did you stop wearing your wedding ring?" Michael looked down at her left hand.

Taryn didn't want to tell Michael the truthful answer to that question because she was afraid that she would start crying.

"I don't know. It's been a while now." She, too, stared at the spot where her ring once glistened. She could see the tan line, from having rarely ever taken the ring off, had disappeared.

The truth was that Ryan had stolen her wedding ring. She figured he probably pawned it for money to fund his gambling addiction. It was one of the most hurtful things he had done to damage their marriage and the most disrespectful thing Taryn could think of someone doing. She had not forgiven Ryan for it and she didn't know if she ever would.

"There you are. I've been looking for you." Dreya walked outside to where Taryn and Michael were. "Glad to see you've been keeping my friend company. I'm Dreya." She smiled while she extended her hand to Michael to introduce herself.

"It's been my pleasure. It's nice to meet you, Dreya." Michael smiled back. "Taryn, I'm hoping we can keep in touch." He turned his attention back to Taryn.

"We exchanged phone numbers before we left the party. I never heard from Michael after that, and I made a conscious decision not to call him. The night was perfect, and I was grateful to have had a good conversation with a man that wasn't Ryan. It was good to know that there were still decent men out there who I could connect with when I was ready. But I wasn't ready to begin a relationship with anyone. I still needed time to heal from the pain of everything that happened with Ryan."

"And did you heal?" Lisa asked Taryn.

"Some days I feel like I did. Some days I feel like I didn't. Right now, I'm really struggling." Taryn gave an honest answer to her friend's question.

"Well, know that I'm here for you. I love you sis." Lisa reassured Taryn.

"I know. I love you too. Thank you for listening."

They said their goodbyes and hung up. Taryn fell asleep just as the sun was coming up.

CHAPTER 8

Dream Deferred

"Now faith is the substance of things hoped for, the evidence of things not seen." Hebrews 11:1 (NKJV)

As the seasons changed and the years passed, Taryn learned that when she married Ryan and had a child with him, she would never really escape him. Yes, she had a divorce decree somewhere in the courthouse that declared the end of their marriage, but she was eternally connected to Ryan through Damon. That fall day when she walked into the courtroom and the judge granted her the divorce, Taryn was under the impression she had gotten rid of Ryan. She was wrong. She still had to work with Ryan to raise Damon and most times it was an ugly chore. They rarely agreed on what was best for Damon in terms of where he went to high school, or who his friends would be, or what kind of activities he would be involved in.

"School is important, but so are sports. He should play sports in high school." Ryan insisted.

"He goes to school for his education. He can play sports outside of school. Going to a school that focuses on academics will prepare him for college."

"So, will sports and being on a team. He can get a scholarship if he works hard in sports."

"He can also get an academic scholarship if he works hard in his classes."

"You never listened to me, even when we were married. Always disagreeing with me."

"You never gave me anything good to agree with when we were married."

Most of their conversations would be painful reminders of why their marriage ended in divorce. In spite of their disagreement, Taryn's goal was for Damon to be a well-rounded young man. She did her best over the years of his upbringing to make sure that he was involved in church, private music lessons, recreational and competitive sports as well as extracurricular activities at school. Keeping him active was costly. Since Ryan didn't agree with it all, especially church activities, he refused to support any of it. With little financial help from Ryan, it was sometimes difficult, and Taryn had to juggle her finances to make it all work.

As Damon grew into a young man, Taryn sacrificed and worked hard for Damon to have the best life she could provide for him. She went back to school. It took years to complete several degrees and she had taken on considerable student loan debt. She resented that Ryan had not done his part in financially supporting Damon, and she told him every chance she got. She was pissed that Ryan was inconsistent and it annoyed Taryn when Ryan would show up at the most inopportune moments to let her know he was still Damon's father.

"He has some nerve. Taryn had just ended another difficult conversation with Ryan as she entered the kitchen where

Damon was watching television from her bedroom. She shook her head, mad at herself because of the choice she made to marry Ryan.

"What's wrong with you, Mom?" Damon looked away from the television for a moment.

"Be careful who you lay down and make babies with. Everybody shouldn't have access to your body." Taryn looked Damon in the eye as she plopped down in a chair across from him.

"Oh, so you've been talking to Dad again, huh?" Damon shook his head and looked back at the television.

"Mom, I know it's important to marry someone who has the same values as me. Someone who was raised like me…I know, I know, Mom! You say this every time after you talk to Dad!" Damon rolled his eyes and stabbed his eggs with his fork before stuffing them into his mouth.

He got upset when Taryn talked about his dad, and he could always read between the lines even though Taryn didn't mention Ryan. Taryn wanted to make sure Damon understood the importance of choosing his relationships carefully. She always said that linking up with Ryan, while it produced Damon and she was grateful to have her son, was not the best decision she could have made for her life. Thirteen years had passed since the divorce and Damon was now eighteen and getting ready to graduate from high school. Ryan had moved to California to restart his life and pursue an entrepreneurial opportunity for the four years of Damon's high school career. Taryn appreciated that she didn't have to deal with Ryan on a day-to-day basis, but she knew it was hard on their son. He missed his father. Damon did travel from time-to-time to California to spend time with his dad. Ryan found a way to maintain his relationship with his son, it was just not what Taryn wanted it to be. Toward the end of Damon's senior year, Ryan relocated back to DC.

Taryn didn't say anything. She stared out the kitchen window that faced the back yard watching the colorful leaves blow off the trees and fall to the ground. The yard was almost completely covered in red, orange and yellow leaves.

"Let's do some raking later today, okay?" She looked forward to spending some quality time with him.

"Yeah, okay." Damon was agreeable, but he was only half paying attention to what Taryn was saying as he slurped his orange juice and scrolled through his phone.

It was Saturday morning and they weren't in a rush for a change. They didn't have anywhere to be, and she was grateful. Those were the rare moments when she usually decided to have one of the many talks with Damon about life choices now that he was a teenager and old enough to understand. It was hard on Damon now that he was older. Neither of his parents worked as hard to hide the disagreements and often involved him in them.

Damon was the only child for both Taryn and Ryan. This was a blessing and a curse for him. He had all of Taryn's attention and she and Ryan didn't have anyone else between them to argue over. This affected Damon and he was vocal with Taryn about the impact.

"Mom, I don't like it when you talk about my dad or when you two argue. Please stop it." Damon had said this to Taryn so many times over the years.

"Do you tell your dad that when he talks about me? Do you talk to your dad like that Damon?" Taryn would respond to Damon in a childish way with her head tilted to the side, lips poked out.

Damon had learned not to answer Taryn's questions as that usually led to a bigger argument between them. He didn't like to argue with his mother. He would go silent until he couldn't take it anymore and then he would push back on Taryn. Damon was not disrespectful to adults because Taryn had raised him not to be. He was preparing to graduate from high school and was on his way to college when Ryan decided it was time for him to return home from California. Damon was so excited when his father returned and all the two of them wanted to do was hang out with one another. Taryn didn't like it when those visits interfered with Damon's school activities.

"So... who are you taking to the senior prom?" Taryn teased Damon. She was smiling from ear to ear thinking about him getting all dressed up and taking pictures.

"I'm not going. Dad and I are going to hang out and go to a game." Damon casually responded as he reached over to grab the milk and poured some over his cereal.

"What? You're not going? When did you decide this?" Taryn blinked as if something was in both eyes. She hunched her shoulders, throwing her hands in the air. Damon could hear the concern in her voice and see it on her face.

"I was *never* going, Mom. It wasn't something that I *just* decided. You *really* don't know me, Mom." He sarcastically mocked Taryn. He used the same hand gesture, blinked his eyes back at her and wrinkled his forehead as if she should have known this all along.

Taryn was visibly upset. Her eyes searched wildly around the room like she was looking for something. This had to be

Ryan's doing. Since he had moved back in town, Damon was distracted from his senior activities and from enjoying time with his friends as he finished off his last year of high school. Ryan had a way of dominating and demanding attention like a two-year-old child whenever he was around. Damon fell for it every time because he loved and adored his father.

"How dare he show up here like he's been here all the time?" Taryn threw her robe across the room after leaving the breakfast table. "Who does he think he is?"

Taryn was angry with Ryan and she was hurt. She hated that Damon seemed to set aside everything he had worked so hard for the last four years of high school to indulge Ryan. Taryn decided to call Ryan a few days later since she didn't get far with Damon about changing his mind to go to the prom.

"Hey Ryan, how are you?" Taryn tried to seem genuinely concerned so she made small talk with Ryan when he first answered the phone.

"Fine," was all he said.

"The reason for my call is that Damon shared that he doesn't want to go to the prom." Taryn sat down on the bed to listen to Ryan's response.

"Yeah, we talked about it and he doesn't want to go. He said some of his friends aren't going and it's not a big deal to him." Ryan was matter of fact and casual in his response.

"Well, it is a big deal! It's his last year of high school. He's creating memories with his friends and classmates. He will never have this time in his life or opportunity again. I think he should go to his prom and participate in all the senior class activities and he should be with his friends right now." Taryn raised her voice then she immediately took a deep breath and caught herself. It took all the restraint she could muster to lower her voice to a quieter tone as yelling wouldn't get her anywhere with Ryan.

"Thank you for not yelling. Look, he doesn't want to go. It's not a big deal. It's a party where people spend lots of money and waste unnecessary time. Kids don't even remember it after it's over. Not everyone wants to go. I didn't go to my prom and I turned out fine." Ryan laughed condescendingly at Taryn for making such a big deal about it.

"Well, I did go to mine and it is important! His friends are going! He is going! Period." Taryn was definitive as she raised her voice. She wanted to jump through the phone and smack Ryan. She was glad they weren't having the conversation in person. Once again, Ryan had made it about himself but tried to make it about Taryn.

"Taryn, it's not about you. He doesn't want to go. So, leave the boy alone." Ryan raised his voice back at her.

"Look! I realize you didn't go to your prom and it's not important to you. That's fine for you! Damon has always participated in school activities. You don't know that because you haven't been here. You stroll back in his senior year and now all of a sudden, he doesn't want to go to prom. He isn't hanging out with his friends like he used to. He just wants to be under you. You don't think it's strange that an eighteen-year-old boy wants to be with his dad all the time instead of with his friends? It's not healthy, Ryan." Taryn lit into Ryan and dumped everything she had been holding for months as she watched her son transform right before her eyes once Ryan returned.

"Wow! You really are crazy! What's wrong with us spending time together, Taryn? Are you jealous that he doesn't want to be with you all the time? One minute you say I'm not here and I haven't helped in raising my son. The next minute you don't want us to spend any time together. I'm here now. I don't know what you want from me." Ryan lit back into Taryn.

"I want you to go away! That's what I want from you. Just go away! Taryn hit the end button on her phone, threw it across the bed and it landed on the carpeted floor.

Taryn's entire body was shaking, and she began to tear up. It felt as if she was right back in the bad marriage with Ryan even though it had been more than a decade since the divorce. In that moment, all the negative energy that she thought had been resolved came rushing right back to the surface. The hurt, anger, frustration, pride and selfishness had taken over again and all she could do was hang up on Ryan. She didn't want to continue being ugly because she knew she was better than that. She took a step back from the situation.

"God, please forgive me. I don't want this ugliness in my heart toward this man. Lord, I thought I was over this. Please help me Lord." Taryn prayed for a place of peace in this situation. She had a lump in her throat, she was sweating, her stomach was churning, and her heart was racing. "I need to calm down. This can't be healthy." Taryn got control of herself as she took a few deep cleansing breaths.

Prayer always worked to calm her down and it helped her to think more clearly. As she began to process the events of the last few days, she thought about what she could do to convince Damon that it was a mistake not to attend his prom. She came up with a plan to approach things from a different perspective. She reached out to a few of the parents of Damon's close friends to see what their plans were for prom. She had influence and she planned to use it in a strategic way to make sure that Damon didn't miss his prom or any other senior activities. Taryn was not about to let Ryan, or anyone, steal Damon's time with his friends or her opportunity to celebrate with him. Not after all the hard work she had put into Damon.

CHAPTER **9**

Letting Go

"But those who hope in the Lord will renew their strength..." Isaiah 40:31 (NIV)

I t had been three weeks since Taryn and Socar last saw each other. "Why are you working so hard?" Socar steadied both her hands on the table and leaned forward to look Taryn straight in the eye without flinching. "Ryan was right. You are crazy!"

Taryn slumped back in her chair looking away from Socar. She couldn't escape the words that pierced her ears like arrows traveling a thousand miles per hour, leaving them bloody. In a matter of seconds, those words reached Taryn's heart and deeply wounded her soul. Socar's words lingered with Taryn long after they had been spoken out of her mouth. She wanted to strike back, but she respected the words and who they came from. She allowed them to sink in.

Taryn had spent so much time talking to Socar about Ryan and Damon. There were so many little things that would spark memories for Taryn. At work, her boss had shared his disappointment for what he considered "caving in" to close the Abdullah account she was working, even though he said he trusted her. Taryn was pissed. First, he said he wanted the deal closed, then he wanted to complain that she gave up so much of her commission to make it happened. She felt like she couldn't win for losing. That sparked a memory of a time when Ryan threw their finances in her face, like their dried-up bank account was her fault. He said, *I trusted you to make sure our accounts were balanced.* Seriously? Then, Damon had a few friends over without asking her first. She'd come home to a house full of loud, smelly young men playing card games with the television loud in the background. No one was even watching it. That brought her back to Ryan's Friday nights out with his "boys." She became teary-eyed.

Ultimately, Taryn knew Socar was right, but she wasn't ready for that level of honesty. Not just yet. She wanted to sulk a bit more. She wanted sympathy. Socar had little time to waste and she always got right to the point. Taryn loved her for this, but she also hated the way it made her turn into a helpless little girl. She wanted to break down and cry, but she knew Socar was the one person who was never afraid to tell her the truth. She would always make her deal with it, no matter how difficult it was for Taryn. For more than two decades, they had built a solid relationship on truth and honesty. Taryn trusted Socar when she needed advice, a swift kick in the pants, or a good dose of reality and truth.

"Ouch! Why do you always have to do that to me?" Taryn reached over her plate of fish tacos to grab her glass of wine. She took a sip to soothe the sting and she grabbed her chest to let Socar know she was still feeling it. "I mean, can't you just beat around the bush one time?" She twisted her lips as she spoke sarcastically back to Socar. Tears began to well up in her eyes again, but she fought them back as she took a deep breath in, quickly letting it out.

Socar laughed a hearty laugh, "Now, why would I do that? And rob you of the opportunity to put on your big girl pants?" She raised one eyebrow and smiled from ear to ear.

It was dinner time and Taryn and Socar had been sitting in their favorite Mexican restaurant for at least two hours catching up on the current events of each other's lives. The server interrupted their conversation to light the candle on the table. The lights had been dimmed in the restaurant indicating the transition from day to evening. The waitress brought the dinner menu in case they wanted to order something. They were both silent for a few minutes thinking about all that had been shared between them.

"Taryn, why don't you go away for a little while to clear your head? It always helps me when I can get away for a little while. Can you take a few days off and do that for yourself?" Socar lovingly interrupted the silence to make a suggestion she believed would help Taryn. She knew Taryn well enough to know she needed to take a break.

"Yes, I think I could do that." Taryn shared with Socar what changes she would need to make in her schedule, where she wanted to go and who she would take with her.

"This time go by yourself. You need some time to think and pray. Let God speak to your heart. You have to do this one alone, sweetie." Socar was right again and Taryn knew it.

"As much as that scares me, you're right. I do need time alone to sort all this out." Taryn looked down at her empty plate and glass and realized that's how she felt inside - empty.

She usually traveled with Damon or her close friends, so this would be totally different for her. She had only traveled alone when she went home to visit her family. She thought of Damon and quickly remembered that Ryan was back in town. Damon would be fine with Ryan. Damon was a young adult who would be going off to college in a few months, anyway. Taryn didn't need to manage his every move. That was clear. She decided she would go to the beach for a few days. Being near the water was Taryn's peaceful place. She was aware of God's presence most when she was at the beach. She knew the exact place she would go. It was about two hours away and the drive would give her some time to think about things.

The next day at work, Taryn worked with Lindsey to clear her calendar of all of her meetings.

"I'll be taking this Thursday and Friday off to make it a long weekend trip. Please make me a reservation at the Hilton Suites in Ocean City for three nights."

"Yes ma'am. Is there anything else?"

"No, thank you. That will be all."

Lindsey came in a few minutes later and gave Taryn the information for her hotel. That night, Taryn began to pack for her trip and sent out a text to her family and close friends letting them know she would be out of town a few days. Damon came in while she was packing.

"Hey Mom! Where you going?" He leaned against the wall facing her bed.

"I'm going to Ocean City for a few days."

"Oh, another business trip?"

"No, I just need to clear my mind and get away for a few days." Taryn continued packing as she talked with her son.

"Oh, who's going with you?"

"I'm going by myself. I need a little time to myself to think."

"You never go anywhere by yourself. Is everything okay?"

"Yes son, everything is okay. I just need to figure out a few things." Taryn stopped packing and sat on the edge of her bed to face Damon.

"I can come with you. I don't have a lot going on at school right now. Are you sure you want to go by yourself?" He questioned his mother. The concern in his voice was like that of a little child worried about his mommy.

"Yes, I'm sure. But thank you. Besides, you're going to be going away to college in a few months. I have to get used to being by myself."

"You're right. Well, when are you leaving?"

"In the morning. I'll still be here before you leave for school."

"Oh! I was staying at Dad's tonight. I just came to get some clothes."

"Okay! Enjoy your time with your dad. I'll let you know when I get there tomorrow."

"When are you coming back?"

"I'll be back Sunday," she smiled as she resumed her packing.

"Okay Mom! You enjoy your trip. Try to relax. You've seemed a little more stressed lately than usual. So, you need this trip for sure. I love you."

"Love you too, Son." Damon gave Taryn a big hug and squeezed her a little tighter than usual before he walked out of her bedroom.

Taryn finished packing making sure to put her favorite journal and a few books she was reading in her beach bag. She took a shower and went to bed to prepare for the drive the next day.

Taryn got up early the next morning, filled her gas tank and drove the two hours to the resort in Ocean City, Maryland. She listened to all her favorite tunes as she enjoyed the bright sunshine and mild temperatures. It was late April and the weather was perfect for the trip. Taryn enjoyed the music, the sun, and the scenery along the way. Once she arrived where she would be staying for the next few days, she would have plenty of time alone to think and pray. She turned onto the road that faced the beach, and she exhaled a sigh. The first sight of the big body of blue water just ahead of her caused a calm to come over her. This trip would be a much-needed relief from the stressors of her life. It didn't matter how many times she had been to the beach, every time she would finally see that large body of water, her soul would be at peace. The very sight of it reminded her that God was amazing and that He was in control. She turned off the busy main street into the circular driveway of the resort. She was met by the valet who opened her car door.

"Good afternoon ma'am. Will you be staying with us?" The handsome young man with blonde hair and rosy cheeks offered her his hand as she stepped out of her car.

"Yes, I will! Thank you so much." She grabbed the ticket from his hand as they headed around to the trunk of the car to get her bags.

Another young man immediately arrived with a cart and assisted Taryn as she took her bags from the car. She watched as her car disappeared out of sight.

The resort was just as beautifully maintained as Taryn remembered. The concierge was near the entrance and warmly greeted Taryn welcoming her to come on in. The white and gray marble floors were shining, and dark cherry wood accents were in all of the furniture and adornments. In the middle of the floor was this large bouquet of live flowers of various kinds that gave off a sweet aroma and blessed her senses. She approached the check in area where two people were waiting to assist her.

"Good afternoon ma'am and welcome. Are you checking in with us today?' The tall slender gentleman reached over to shake her hand.

"Yes, thank you. My name is Taryn Madrid." She searched her purse for her wallet to supply him with her driver's license and credit card.

The man found her reservation and quickly checked her in.

"Ok, Ms. Madrid, you are on the seventeenth floor in room seventeen hundred." He showed Taryn the key card with her room number written on it.

He went on to explain about breakfast, Happy Hour, where the gym and pool areas were and how she could access the beach from different doorways leading out of the resort. Taryn listened because it had been a while since she had been there. Usually she would never pay attention to such details as she always traveled with someone who was more interested in those small details, and she could just ask them. Since she was alone this time, she needed to manage her details on her own. The young man was standing close by with her bags and he let her know he was taking her bags up to her room.

"You are free to explore the hotel and your bags will be in your room waiting for you when you arrive there." He was wheeling the cart toward the elevator as Taryn thanked him and handed him a five-dollar bill.

She forgot to tip the valet driver and she went to find him to give him a tip. She didn't find him, but she got excited when she saw the indoor pool and spa area. She would definitely schedule a massage while she was there. She could see people out on the beach even though it wasn't warm enough to get in the water. She went up to her room to unpack her suitcase and get settled in her room. As she unlocked the door to her room and stepped in, she saw the curtains covering the wall of windows and the sliding glass doors were open. She could see a full view of the ocean. It was an absolutely breathtaking view.

"Thank you, God." She whispered a tiny prayer and headed straight for the balcony to take it all in.

She stood on the balcony for a while then decided to head to the beach to watch the sun set. She changed into her flip flops, grabbed her favorite book and her journal. Taryn often read more than one book at a time based on her interests and she enjoyed writing down some of her feelings in her journal. At the moment, she was intrigued with the brain and spirituality and she was reading about how to re-wire the brain using scriptures. It was the perfect information to help her reflect on her trip. She sat on the beach reading until the sun began to dim. Then she watched the sunset. While sitting, she prayed and meditated and closed her eyes to listen to the sound of the waves crashing against one another. It was peaceful, and the saltwater smell filling the air was cleansing to her nostrils. With her eyes closed, she listened intently to the waves and allowed them to speak to her and she whispered a little prayer as the sun kissed her skin as it began setting.

"Thank you, Father for allowing me to be here right now. This is the first time in a long time I've felt balanced and whole.

I know everything is going to be alright. With a little prodding, I know I can convince Damon to attend his prom. But if he doesn't go, it will be alright. I release it and I surrender it to you. I give myself the gift of forgiveness for engaging in such negative behavior with Ryan. I'm going to let You handle it. I've been trying way too hard to control everything and to be everything to Damon for far too long. I raised him well and it is time for me to let him go. It is time for me to take back my life and figure out what makes me happy again. I'm letting go. I'm letting go." Taryn closed her eyes, breathed in and exhaled as she sat still. She listened to the waves crashing against each other and she whispered to herself over and over again, "I'm letting it all go."

When Taryn opened her eyes, she was surrounded by darkness with only a slither of light from the moon. She had many revelations as she sat meditating and before going back to her room, she decided to stop by the indoor pool where there was light so she could write them down in her journal. In her journal, she wrote...

I arrived at the resort today. It is as beautiful as I remembered. For more than an hour, I sat on the beach listening to my inner voice. It was peaceful and calm, and it was nice to be there by myself. I have never been on a trip by myself, so this was a big step for me. I'm glad I did it. It's good to be alone with yourself sometimes. I also realize it's good to have someone by your side to experience life with. I think that's why I've been holding on to Damon so tightly...afraid of not having someone to love and care for. I realize that if I die today or tomorrow, the only regret I might have is not having loved again. I don't need a man for the reasons I thought I needed one in the past, but I do want that special one. I have overcome the expectations that others created by putting fear in my heart of not being whole without a man. I am whole all by myself. I understand that now. I no longer subscribe to a narrative that tells me anything different. I now fully understand the power of my own individuality and I completely accept my unique purpose that God gave me when He placed me on this Earth. I know I am bringing a lot to the table, and companionship with a partner who is confident in who he is will only accentuate my journey through life. I know God designed human beings to be with one another to share love and relationship. I believe I can accomplish far more with another person than by myself. I also know that loving someone else will challenge me to be unselfish and I will have to grow even more. I humbly accept the challenge.

A server came by and asked if she wanted a drink. She ordered an Arnold Palmer. She loved iced lemonade tea. As she sat on a lounge chair poolside sipping her tea and enjoying her mini vacation, Taryn watched a couple playing together in the pool. She smiled as she enjoyed the playfulness and laughter between them. She wrote in her journal again…

What do I value most about the important relationships in my life?

Taryn sat her journal down on a nearby wicker table. The slight smell of chlorine mixed with suntan lotion filled the air as she took a breath. She grabbed her journal and began writing again…

I am excited about the possibility of a new relationship. What have the important people in my life taught me about relationships? The first person that comes to mind is my Grandma Bella. I treasured the honesty and loyalty she displayed for me as a child growing up. Through the years, my mother, Zoah. showed me time and time again what it meant to have integrity. She never let her vulnerabilities and mistakes stop her. She always worked hard, and she sacrificed for our family. Then there's Socar. I'm so glad she suggested I come on this trip. Socar will hold me accountable when I'm wrong yet do it in the most direct, loving and kind way. Lastly, I desire someone in my life that will be fully committed to me like my dad, Evan, has been over the years. He has always supported all of my wildest dreams and aspirations. That's what I value... honesty, integrity, loyalty, trust and commitment.

Taryn closed her journal and when she was finished with her tea, she slowly strolled into the building and approached the elevators to go back to her room. The elevator doors opened, and a young couple stepped off. They were holding hands and the guy had two beach chairs thrown over his shoulder. They were laughing and seemed to be having a great time with one another as they passed her. Taryn looked them both in the eye and smiled at them. The sight of the happy couple made her dream of the new person that God would eventually put in her life. It was fun and exciting to think about a new relationship. Yet, she knew she would have to be patient with the process.

Over the next few days Taryn spent at the resort; she got that massage she wanted. She shopped a little and also enjoyed several oceanside dinners. She called Damon to check in with him and apologize for her part in the disagreements they had been having.

"Hey Son! How are you?" Taryn was excited to hear Damon's voice.

"I'm good Mom! How are you? Are you enjoying your trip?" Damon was excited to hear his mom's voice, too.

"I am really enjoying it. It was just what I needed. I've been so relaxed and able to think. I've been doing some reflecting. It's been good for me to be alone to do that, and I want to tell you something." Taryn paused to let Damon respond.

"Okay! Is everything alright?" Damon sounded concerned.

Taryn laughed. "Yes, everything is okay, Son. I just have a few things I need to share with you. I want you to know I realize how difficult I have made things between me and you. That also includes your Dad. I'm sorry. I hope you can forgive me." Tears welled up in Taryn's eyes.

"Of course, I forgive you. I'm not sure I understand what has come over you, but I'm glad to hear your apology. Is this for real?" Damon laughed to break the seriousness of the moment.

"Yes Son, it's for real. I'm sorry for things I've said and done. I'm going to work to make things different between us when I get back home. Our relationship is one of the most important things in my life and I don't ever want to harm it again." Taryn spoke sincerely to Damon.

"Wow! I really appreciate you for saying all this. It means a lot to me. I needed to hear this, Mom." Damon was grateful.

"I love you! I'm so proud of you and so thankful you're my son." Taryn prepared to end the conversation.

"I love you too, Mom. I'm looking forward to seeing you when you get home." Damon was smiling.

"Alright, goodbye sweetie."

"Bye Mom!" Damon ended the call.

Taryn rested and continued to reflect by writing in her journal. On her last day as she was preparing to leave, she wrote her final journal entry...

As I prepare to return home, I wonder what I need to do to be different? I know God does not always move quickly. The heart takes time to heal.

Taryn rolled each piece of clothing and tightly packed everything back into her suitcase as she prepared to leave the resort to return home.

Once she was settled in the car as she drove home with the sun beaming down through the open sunroof of her car, she called Socar.

"Hey lady, how was your trip?" Socar answered the phone after the first ring as if she was waiting for Taryn to call.

"It was great! Thank you so much for making me take this trip. I really needed to get away." Taryn focused her eyes on the road while talking through the Bluetooth in her car.

"I'm so glad to hear it. Nothing like some time alone to help you figure things out."

"Ain't that the truth. I made a deal with myself to balance my excitement about the future with a healthy dose of reality. I am extremely clear that I still have work to do on myself. I don't want to skip that important part of the process. I am leaving old things behind and becoming open to love again. Once I am ready to receive him, there is no doubt in my mind that God will entrust me with a new love." Taryn shared one of the major revelations she had while on her trip.

"Sounds like we have work to do to prepare you for that." Socar laughed and told Taryn what books on relationships she should read first.

Over the next year, Taryn focused on loving herself and learning more about building healthy relationships. She enjoyed time with her family and friends, and she was more intentional about being present in the moments and not wondering when she was going to find love again. She put her time and energy into reading books on relationships to learn more about what she didn't know that had been detrimental to her in her marriage to Ryan.

Taryn invited her friends and family – Zoah, Socar, Yanna, Lisa and Dreya - to form a book club and join her in reading the books Socar recommended. She also invited her friend, NaVon Lee, who she had grown close to since their sons played on the same sports team. One day at practice NaVon saw Taryn reading one of the books and asked about it. They started a conversation and NaVon got the book and started reading it. She and Taryn had some conversation about the book, but they were both looking forward to the larger discussion with the other ladies. Since they were all in different parts of the country, they agreed to meet monthly by conference call to discuss what they were reading so they could process the information together. All the ladies joined their first conference call.

"Hello ladies! Thank you all for joining the discussion tonight. I'm so excited that you all dialed in this evening. Let's have a roll call. Who do we have on here?"

"Hello ladies! I'll go first. My name is Zoah. I'm Taryn's mother."

"Hello Ms. Zoah. How are you?" The ladies chimed in one by one.

"Hi ladies, I'm Dreya and I work with Taryn. Excited to be here tonight."

"My name is Yanna and I'm Taryn's big sister, and I've been looking forward to this call all day. Can't wait to get started."

"Hello my dear sisters! My name is Socar and I have been mentoring Taryn for a long time. She's one of my many adopted daughters." Socar laughed at herself. There were a countless number of people she mentored and adopted over her adult life.

"Hi everyone! My name is Lisa, and Taryn and I were college roommates. We also went to high school together, so I've known her a long time."

"I'm NaVon. I've probably known Taryn the shortest time, but I feel like I've known her forever. We met a few years ago when our sons played on the high school basketball team together, and we became instant friends. We just clicked. She's my sister, friend and confidant. We've shared a lot of good times and conversations at my house. I appreciate our friendship so much, and I'm grateful to meet all of you over the phone today and hope to meet you all in person soon." NaVon was gracious as always.

"Ok ladies, so we don't really have a protocol for how these calls will go. We just wanted to get together and share our a-ha's from what we are reading. All of us are at different places in our lives with relationships. Some are married, some of us are divorced and some have never been married before. With that said, anyone can start. Who wants to go first?" Taryn opened the line for the ladies to chime into the conversation. There was at least thirty seconds of silence before Zoah spoke.

"Well, I want to say that as I've been reading some of the information. It's nothing new, but it's always good to be reminded of these things. When you have lived as long as I have and had relationships, you learn a lot by trial and error. It's good to know that there are books out here that younger women can read today to learn some of these things and avoid making mistakes that maybe we all have made."

"Mom if this isn't anything new, why didn't you ever tell me and Taryn these things?" Yanna asked Zoah. "Not trying to be disrespectful but I mean…I feel like some of this is definitely conversation we should've had. I'm curious about that."

"I didn't know how to put some of this into words. When you're raising kids, you do the best you can with the information you have. That's why I said I'm glad this information is out here now and you all as younger women can access it. I'm not sure my generation had the opportunity to learn about the perspective that's presented here. We were a product of the women's liberation movement where women were not supposed to submit to a man. We were taught to be independent of a man. That's what my mother taught me and that's what I taught you all. I can acknowledge there was some middle ground that should have been explored that may have made things a little easier." Zoah acknowledged what she didn't know.

Socar chimed in. "I can agree with Zoah. I'm a part of her generation and I can assure you that we were not taught these things. Some of this was new information for me but a lot of it wasn't new, it just wasn't something we discussed or were taught to discuss with our children."

The conversation continued for more than forty-five minutes with a rich discussion about the different points in the book, *Love and Respect,* by Dr. Emerson Eggerichs. There was a healthy debate about what it meant to submit and allow a man to lead in a relationship. All of the women approached the topic from their various experiences and perspectives.

"I struggled with much of what I read here. I will submit, but not to foolishness. You've got to give me something substantial to submit to. I mean…I'll work with you…but…where are we going? What are we doing?" Dreya wasn't budging on her expectations of the role of a man.

"But don't you think the lines have been blurred today? You have men taking on more non-traditional roles and women doing the same. I don't think it's as easy as it was back in the day when traditional roles were the expectation for men and women. I've been with my husband a long time and we had to work through that as he came into the marriage with expectations, and so did I. Some of those expectations worked for us and others didn't. It took a lot of communication and compromise to figure out what works for us." NaVon shared her experience.

"NaVon, I agree with you. My husband and I have had to find a place that works for us. With raising kids and both of us working to make our household work, we have had to learn it's all about give and take." Lisa had listened long enough until she was comfortable sharing.

"Ladies, I feel you. Marriage for me and my husband has been all about give and take." Yanna added her two cents.

"Ok ladies, thanks for a great discussion. As we wrap up… if you had to pick one thing that stood out to you in the book or from our discussion today, what would it be?" Taryn focused the group.

Each woman took the opportunity to share her revelation with the group and Taryn summarized for them.

"So, if I had to say what I hear as a theme in all of what has been shared is, it takes a lot of patience, flexibility, love and forgiveness to start each new day together when you finally find your lifelong partner. Do I have that correct?" Taryn did a consensus check.

"Yes, that would pretty much sum it up." Yanna's voice rose above the rest, but they all responded in agreement, some in unison.

Thank you for sharing, ladies. I'll be following up with each of you, and I look forward to our call next month. Until then, let's put into practice what we have learned and be a blessing!"

Taryn ended the call and sat in her window seat for a minute to write in her journal and process all she had heard. The phone rang after about forty-five minutes had passed. It was Socar.

"Hey, that was a wonderful conversation. I need to process it more. Do you want to get together for dinner in an hour and we can continue it?"

"Yes, I would really like that. Legal Seafood okay with you?"

"Yes, that's a favorite! That's perfect! See you in an hour."

Taryn and Socar spent the evening eating dinner at the restaurant and sharing their insights about the book discussion.

"So, men are just as vulnerable as women. I think we all realize this now." Taryn sat across from Socar at dinner enjoying the crab dip appetizer they ordered before the entrees.

"Yes, probably more so than women. They don't really have an outlet to show those vulnerabilities, so it comes out in different unhealthy ways." Socar shook her head. "We as women tend to bear the burden of that because we are usually the closest ones to them."

"So many new things to learn. I wish I had known some of this stuff back when I was married. The point about how men thrive on respect and women on love. I thought love was most important to men, too." Taryn chewed the food she had put in her mouth.

"Nope, men are different. They need respect first in order to feel loved. We need to be told and shown we are loved on a daily basis." Socar took a sip of water.

They continued talking while they finished dinner and left the restaurant with a plan to continue holding the monthly discussions with the women and seeking more books to read on relationships. They also made a commitment to add prayer and meditating on Bible scriptures on relationships to their daily routine.

More than a year passed, and Taryn was feeling strong. She began working out and eating healthy. She was looking and feeling great. For the first time in a long time, Taryn was happy. She was living a wonderful life. That's when she met Aman Eniale.

CHAPTER **10**

To Be His Friend

"Love is patient. Love is kind. It does not envy, it does not boast, it is not proud." 1 Corinthians 13:4 (NIV)

Until Taryn met Aman, she only thought she had been in love before. She had different information now about what it meant to be in an intimate relationship with another human being. That new understanding created a different kind of appreciation and respect for men in general and a sweeter love in her heart that she was ready to share when Aman came along.

Taryn first met Aman through her friend NaVon and her husband, Thomas. It was Christmas Day and Taryn decided to accept the invite to spend the day with her friends. Damon was spending the day with Ryan, and Taryn was relieved she had some place to go since she didn't travel home to be with her family in Louisiana. She didn't want to travel home without Damon this year. It was always kind of awkward when she went home without him. Her family and friends back home loved and adored Damon and always wanted to see them both. People would ask where he was, and she would have to explain that he was with his dad. Taryn wasn't in the mood to constantly have to explain where he was and deal with the discomfort that came after their barrage of questions. It was difficult enough not having him with her for the holidays. She was grateful for the invite from NaVon and Thomas to spend the day at their house.

When she arrived, Aman was in the kitchen helping to set things up for the annual brunch that Thomas and NaVon held each Christmas Day at their home. They would bring friends together from near and far to celebrate, to catch up on life events and to talk about love, relationships and everything else in between. The guys would usually gather in one part of the house, usually the basement, while the ladies would convene in the kitchen and family room. Everyone would naturally come together to share a larger conversation by the end of the day, that usually ran into the evening hours.

NaVon and Thomas were welcoming of everyone and they went to great lengths to make their home warm and inviting. It was a place where she could really relax. They were a great example of how two people could successfully partner in marriage, and Taryn admired their relationship and hoped to have that special love in her life someday. Taryn had a dish that she had made to contribute to the food, and she headed to the kitchen to drop it off. That's where she first saw Aman.

"Whoa! Who is that beautiful person?" Taryn mumbled to NaVon as her eyes danced across the kitchen and locked in on Aman. She quickly looked away as she placed the dish on the center island in the kitchen. She continued to say hello and give out hugs to the people she knew.

"That's Aman, he's Thomas' friend from school. He's divorced, but I think he might be dating someone."

"Aren't they always." Taryn was disappointed, but still happy to behold such a cutie.

The sight of Aman almost knocked the wind out of Taryn. Aman was six feet four inches tall and he reminded Taryn of her dad, Evan. He had a smooth dark chocolate flawless complexion. His broad shoulders and bulging biceps made it impossible to miss him in any room. He had little body fat, which made the muscles throughout his entire body pop. The loose curly black hair on his head beckoned for Taryn to run her fingers through it. His beard and goatee were neatly trimmed and cut with precision. Aman was a stylish dresser and he smelled good. He was well put together. Taryn loved his style. She didn't expect to see anyone so handsome at that moment. There was an instantaneous attraction between the two of them. NaVon introduced them and when they reached out to shake hands, Taryn knew she was in trouble when they touched one another. There were only a few times in her life that she had felt that kind of spark from meeting someone new.

"Wow, rough hands. You must be good with those." Even though NaVon told Taryn Aman was divorced, Taryn still looked at his hand for a wedding ring, just in case. When she didn't see a ring, she intentionally looked Aman in the eye for three seconds longer than she normally would have before giving him her signature smile that lit up the room.

"Yes ma'am, I can do a few things well." Aman raised his left eyebrow higher than the right. He returned the stare, looking deeply into Taryn's eyes while he slowly shook his head up and down.

Taryn could see by the way his eyes danced over her body that he was in full agreement with the natural connection they were both feeling. As the day went on, they shared brief glances and conversation. Taryn learned a little more about Aman. He was divorced and he had a teenage daughter. He was also in a relationship.

"Shoot! The good ones are always taken." Taryn sighed in disappointment. She decided she would enjoy the day and being in the company of all the amazing people in her presence. There was laughter and joy that created memorable moments throughout the day, and Taryn was grateful for everything the day taught her. Even though Taryn wanted to keep in touch with Aman, she respected that he was in a relationship. He did not ask her for her number either. Taryn put Aman out of her mind and focused on her life.

A few years passed before Aman and Taryn both attended the annual Christmas brunch again. This time, Aman had ended his relationship. Taryn had dated, but she was not in a serious relationship with anyone. The timing was perfect, and Taryn was excited to connect with Aman again. It was as if no time had passed at all. They spent the day talking and sharing with one another. This time, Aman was very attentive to Taryn and there was no stopping what was inevitably ahead in their future.

"How have you been? I haven't seen you in a while." Aman was kneeling on one knee in front of Taryn.

"I know right! I haven't been here in a few years. I've been good. What about you?' Taryn smiled and returned the pleasantry.

They chatted for hours about work, their children and life. At the end of it, Aman asked her for her phone number.

"So, how do I keep in touch with you?" Aman looked her in the eye as he handed her his business card with his information on it.

"Um, here's my information. I look forward to speaking with you more. I want you to call me when you're ready. I don't want you to feel any pressure at all." Taryn handed Aman her business card in return.

The two exchanged a hug as they prepared to leave the brunch. Taryn was smiling showing all of her teeth because, by the way her stared at her, it was clear Aman was interested.

Taryn held Aman's phone number for more than a week before she called him one Monday morning. She spent that time praying and meditating to make sure she felt good in her soul about calling him.

"Hello, good morning! This is Taryn. How are you? Did I catch you at a good time?" Taryn was in the car on her way to work.

"Hi Taryn! Yes, this is a great time. I was wondering if you would call. I was going to give you a few more days before I called you. I was really trying not to be pressed, but I didn't want to miss another opportunity to get to know you better." Aman laughed.

"Oh really! You didn't think I would call?" Taryn probed more.

"I wasn't sure. Sometimes women say they will call just to be nice. You never hear from them again." Aman shared his experience with Taryn.

"One thing you will learn about me…if I say I'm going to do something…I'm going to do it. Otherwise…I don't say it." She was direct with Aman.

"Ok, I can appreciate that. Let me know where you're coming from, mama." Aman chuckled at Taryn's direct tone.

"So, what is it that you do exactly? I know you said you work for the government." Taryn asked in a curious tone.

"Yes, I work for the federal government. I'm a contractor. I have the highest security clearance, and I do whatever they tell me to do." Aman was vague.

"Ok, so you're one of *those* people?" Taryn rolled her eyes up in her head when she spoke.

"What do you mean *those* people?" Aman sounded slightly offended.

"You know the people who *claim* their job is so important that they can't talk about it?" Taryn added air quotes. "Please!"

"Well ma'am…I will have you know that my job is that important and I can't talk about it. I can assure you I don't do anything illegal. I ain't going to jail for nobody and definitely not for a job." Aman was serious for a moment.

"Ok, I hear you. I'll leave it alone for now." Taryn had enough information to be dangerous.

"So…Ms. Madrid…when can a brother take you out? Breakfast, lunch or dinner, which would you prefer?"

"My days are so hectic; I would have to opt for dinner. Breakfast is sketchy and lunch…who has time for lunch?" Taryn laughed and shrugged her shoulders.

"Breakfast is one of the most important meals of the day… but dinner it is. How about dinner and a movie this Friday night?" Aman proposed a date.

"Sure! It's been a while since I've been out on a date on a Friday night. That would be nice. I would like that." Taryn chuckled thinking back to all the Friday nights she missed going out when she was married to Ryan.

Taryn and Aman talked every morning that week leading up to their first date. They talked about politics, current events, sports, music, religion and relationships.

Aman was well-educated and more refined than any man she had dated. He was intellectual and could hold a shallow or deep conversation about any topic, and he wasn't afraid to express himself. Taryn loved this and she appreciated him as she got to know more about his views of the world.

When Aman arrived to pick up Taryn for their first date, she asked Damon to answer the door. Damon agreed because he wanted to see who was taking his mom out.

The doorbell rang and Damon answered.

"How you doing young man? Is Taryn here?" Aman was dressed casually as they were going to dinner and a movie.

"Yes sir, she is. Come on in." Damon admired Aman's sneakers.

"I'm Aman."

"Good to meet you Mr. Aman. I'm Dame." They shook hands.

"Nice shoes!" Aman pointed to Damon's vintage red and blue Michael Jordan sneakers.

"Man, I was just about to say the same thing about your shoes." They both laughed.

"Yeah, I have a nephew, a little older than you, and he keeps me in the latest kicks. We play basketball sometimes. Maybe you can join us. Your mom says you like to play." Aman wanted to connect with Damon.

"Yeah, my dad and I play, too. That's actually where I'm headed right now. I'm meeting him to shoot some hoops." Damon palmed the basketball that was sitting on the floor next to the couch and smacked it while he tossed it back and forth in his hands.

"Cool. That's what's up." Aman looked around at the pictures Taryn had framed of her and Damon over the years. He could see they had a strong bond.

"You can have a seat in the living room if you like. I'll let my mom know you're here. Can I get you anything to drink?" Taryn had passed on her southern values to Damon, and he knew to offer guests something to drink when they visited the house.

"No, I'm good. Thank you though." Aman was pleasantly surprised at Damon's hospitality. On his last few dates, the young people he encountered had not been as welcoming or polite. It was evident Taryn had invested a lot in this young man.

Damon ran upstairs, knocked on the door and stepped into Taryn's bedroom when she yelled, "Come in" from the bathroom.

"Your date is here." Damon shouted into the open bathroom door.

Taryn appeared and walked through the door toward Damon. "Thank you, babe. What do you think?" Taryn was whispering as if someone could hear her.

"You look great Mom. You always do." Damon grabbed Taryn and gave her a big hug and a kiss on the cheek.

"I wasn't talking about me. But, thank you son. I was talking about Aman. What do you think about him?"

"Oh, he seems cool. He seems like a nice enough guy." Damon shrugged nonchalantly.

"That's it! That's all you have to say?" Taryn smiled and shrugged her shoulders mocking him.

"Pretty much. I'm going to play basketball with Dad. I'll probably stay over with him tonight. He's hasn't been feeling well lately. Have fun on your date and be safe." Damon hugged Taryn again and quickly disappeared before she could ask him what he meant about Ryan not feeling well lately.

"Oh well, I'll ask him about that later." Taryn paused for a minute and looked up at the ceiling before she went back to the bathroom to check her hair and outfit one last time before Aman would see her.

Damon addressed Aman on his way out. "My mom will be ready in a minute."

"Ok, thank you." Aman was standing near Taryn's favorite window seat looking out at the beautiful sun that was quickly setting.

"It was nice to meet you, sir. Have fun tonight and take good care of my mom. She's incredibly special to me." Damon locked eyes with Aman to let him know he was dead serious, and he extended his right hand to shake Aman's hand.

"I definitely will. Nice to meet you, too." Aman extended his hand back to Damon. He was surprised once again at Damon's good manners.

Shortly after, Taryn stepped into the living room. Aman's back was turned, and he didn't hear her come in.

"Hey, how are you?" Taryn walked over to him as he turned toward her.

"I'm great now that you are ready to go. You look amazing." Aman stood back to check out Taryn before he gave her a hug.

"Thank you! You look great, too. I'm ready to go." She grabbed her jacket to put it on.

He came up from behind to assist her with her jacket. "Your son told me to take good care of you and that's exactly what I intend to do."

On the first date, Taryn noticed that Aman was the kind of man who opened doors and pulled out chairs. He appeared to be a gentleman. Taryn appreciated this as she had never dated a man who did these things. She had been so accustomed to doing everything herself. Aman told her to relax and let him take care of her. It was what Taryn wanted, and for once in a long time, she let her guard down. She trusted Aman. It was as if he could see some of the things that she had been missing in her life. Conversation with him was easy.

"It's so nice to be out on a date on a Friday night. It's been a long time since I've had one."

"Really, you seem like you would have plenty of guys trying to take you out."

"It's not because I couldn't have gone out, I just didn't find anyone who I was interested in until now."

"Oh well…that's a lot of pressure for a brother. I hope I can live up to your expectations." Aman raised both hands in the air.

"Well, you're already off to a great start so far."

Aman smiled and reached over and put his hand on Taryn's. It felt good and Taryn turned her wrist up to lock her fingers with Aman's. They both held on tightly as they rode the rest of the way to the restaurant in silence. Taryn rested her head on the headrest. She couldn't believe she had finally met the man she had waited and prayed for. Once they arrived at the Bahama Breeze restaurant and were seated, Aman ordered food and drinks for them.

"Let me test my skill to see if I've been listening to what you like."

"Okay. I can order for myself you know."

"Of course, you can, but let me see if I can get this right."

"She will have the fish tacos, with extra guacamole and a Cuervo Margarita on the rocks with salt."

The waitress looked at Taryn to confirm. She nodded at her in confirmation.

"Yes Boo, you nailed it." Taryn gave Aman a high five. She was smiling ear to ear.

"Okay, I'll have the jerk wings with rice and peas, plantains and a side salad. And I'll have a Mango Mojito to drink."

The waitress put their order in and returned shortly with their drinks. As they sipped their cocktails, they talked about places they had traveled to in the Caribbean and places they still wanted to experience.

"I love the water. It's my place of peace. I grew up visiting my dad's family in Florida every summer. I learned to love the beach."

"I like the water, but I'm not a fan of the sun. I like looking at the water from a cool spot inside." Aman chuckled.

"Yeah, I like looking at it too, but I also like getting in the water. It's fun!"

"I can't wait to take a trip with you. I think you would be a great travel companion." Aman pointed at Taryn.

"Yeah, I know how to have a little fun." She shimmied her shoulders.

"I bet you do. You like to dance?"

"Absolutely! I love to dance." Taryn moved her hands back and forth.

"Okay, we'll go dancing on our next date."

"Okay, that sounds like fun."

"Already planning our next date, huh?" Taryn playfully raised an eyebrow.

"Yeah, I think you're good for at least two dates." Aman held up two fingers.

As the two of them were laughing at his comment, their food arrived. The waitress placed the food in front of them and disappeared after she made sure they didn't need anything.

"So, let's go a little deeper." Taryn chewed the food she had just put in her mouth.

"Okay, how do we do that?"

I'll say two words and you choose one and tell me why you chose it."

"Okay, I don't think I've ever played this game before, but I'm interested." Aman shook his head.

"Love or respect?"

"Respect for sure. Respect is the foundation of real, true love."

"Okay, that makes sense."

"Fire or ice?"

"Not sure what you mean by this one." Aman tilted his head to the right side.

"What comes to mind first?"

"Well fire makes me think of passion and I'm all for that. But ice makes me think of being calm and cool under pressure and that's necessary too. I'm gonna go with ice."

"Okay, I like that."

"Can I give you one?"

"Yes, let's see what you got."

"Open or closed?" Aman fired.

"Definitely open. To me open means freedom. I always say I'm an open book. I'm free to share my life." Taryn opened her arms wide.

"Okay, okay. Makes sense. First or last?" Aman held up one finger.

"First means you can blaze a trail, but last means you can perfect what's been done. I'm gonna go with last."

"Really, I'm impressed. I thought you would've said first."

"I would've years ago, but a little wisdom has allowed me to understand the benefit of sitting back to observe and going last."

Aman checked his watch and it was nine o'clock, "Okay, I'm going to let that sink in for a minute as we finish our food. The movie starts at nine thirty. We have thirty minutes."

They finished eating, and Aman asked for the check and paid it. The movie theater was a short distance across the parking lot. They walked over and continued talking. They arrived at the theater and Aman bought tickets to see the newest James Bond movie that had just come out.

"I love action movies, especially James Bond movies. I've been wanting to see this one." Taryn had a look on her face like a kid.

"Me too. Hope it's a good one."

They found their seats and snuggled in next to one another. Throughout the movie, Taryn rested her head on Aman's shoulder very naturally. During a love scene in the movie, Aman squeezed Taryn's hand a little tighter and she squeezed back. After the movie, on the drive home, they chatted about their favorite scenes from the movie and compared previous versions. Neither of them wanted the night to end, but Taryn had a yoga class scheduled at a new studio the next morning. Aman pulled up to her house and parked in the driveway.

"Thank you so much for an amazing evening. I had such a great time. Looking forward to the next one." Taryn looked him in the eye.

"You're welcome. It was my pleasure and I'm also looking forward to it. Let me walk you to the door."

Aman came around and opened Taryn's car door to let her out. Taryn waited for him.

"I could get used to this." Taryn laughed.

"You had better. This is how we rollin' from now on." Aman grabbed her hand to help her out the car and walked her to the door. He waited for her to find her keys.

"Thank you again and good night." Taryn reached for a hug.

Aman gave her a bear hug with a gentle squeeze and kissed her on the cheek.

"Good night. Can I call you in the morning?"

"You better!" Taryn opened the door and stepped inside. She leaned her head against the door and thanked God for sending her Aman.

The next morning, Aman called Taryn before her yoga class.

"I had a really good time last night. What about you?"

"I did too. It was so much fun. It was absolutely perfect." Taryn got up, dressed for class, grabbed her yoga mat and drove to the studio. They talked until she got there and after she left.

From that very first date, when the two weren't together, they were talking to each other several times throughout the day. They developed a bond very quickly and it wasn't long before they were spending most evenings together. Taryn had already decided she wanted to make love to Aman. It was just a matter of time. Over the next month, Aman took his time with Taryn and invited her slowly into his world, but he never let her in all the way. There was something about Aman that Taryn couldn't quite put her finger on, but she was already emotionally involved by that time. Aman was the first man to inspire Taryn in a way that no man ever had.

"Hey good morning, beautiful! How are you today?" Aman called Taryn on his way to work.

"Good morning, handsome. I'm good. How are you?" Taryn yawned and rubbed her eyes.

"Are you ready for a new day? You get to be brilliant today. How will you use all the gifts God gave you today? Who will you impact today?" Aman fired questions Taryn's way and didn't wait for a response in between.

"Yes! Yes! I'm ready for the day. Leave it to you to challenge me with all those other questions. Let me think about all that for a minute. Why are you so happy early this morning?" Taryn stretched as she rolled out of the bed to the floor. She headed to the bathroom.

"Just thankful to be alive another day. Grateful to have so many beautiful people like you in my life. The sun is shining. Life is good." Aman was definitely in an infectious mood.

"Well, Mr. Sunshine, thank you for waking me up and sharing your joy this morning. I'm grateful to have you in my life as well and I will work on being all that I can be today. Will you allow me to take you out to dinner tonight? I can answer your questions then." Taryn reciprocated with a gesture of kindness.

"You're gonna take me out? Did I hear that right?" Aman laughed and asked to be sure.

"Yes, I'd like to take you out tonight. Where would you like to go? And it doesn't have to be Checkers. I know that's one of your favorites." Taryn chuckled at Aman.

He rarely ever ate fast food, but when he did crave it, he always wanted Checkers.

"Wow, I really appreciate that. I don't know if a woman has ever asked or actually taken me out. This is a first for me. Ms. Madrid, you are changing the game, Love." Aman laughed but he was serious.

"You've taken me out for a month, and I want you to know that I appreciate you. It's a little something I can do to let you know how much. So, think about where you want to go and text me later today. We will go after work. Is that okay with you?" Taryn could tell Aman was excited to choose the dinner spot because his voice sounded like a little kid on Christmas morning.

"Yes, that's fine with me, and I know where I want to go. I can tell you now." Aman was eager to share.

"Oh really, where do you want to go, Handsome?"

"There's this Cuban spot in the city. They have rooftop dining and salsa dancing. It's going to be a perfect evening for it. I've been wanting us to go and my spirit is telling me this is the night for it." Aman dragged out his words slowly and seductively.

"Oooooo...that sounds like the perfect spot. Dinner and dancing...I could use some of that kind of fun in my life right now." Taryn was getting excited too.

"I can't wait to get you on that dance floor and show you a few of my moves and you can show me what you got, Baby-girl." Aman set the mood for the evening.

"Yes, Mr. Eniale! This is going to be fun. I'll be looking forward to dancing with you all day." Taryn whispered to assure Aman she was up for it.

"I'll see you at six," Aman set the time.

"Yes, you absolutely will." Taryn confirmed.

"Have a great day! Remember to be your brilliant self." Aman reminded Taryn.

"I will. Just for you, my love." Taryn ended the call and danced around in the mirror practicing for the evening.

She went to her closet and pulled out a fitted red dress that hugged every curve of her body especially around her breasts and buttocks. The dress flared a little at the bottom and invited attention with every move she made. She pulled out her cheetah printed red bottom pumps to match. She knew that when Aman saw her in that dress and those shoes, it would be an evening of fire and passion.

Throughout the day, Aman and Taryn exchanged texts that added to the expectation of the evening.

Aman texted, "What are you wearing tonight?"

"Something spicy. You'll love it!" Taryn responded.

"I already do. Can I see?" Aman wanted a preview.

"No. You have to wait. It'll be worth it." Taryn made him wait.

"It always is. Always!" Aman confirmed his passion for her.

That night, they had a wonderful meal and danced the night away. The energy between them was electric as they flirted with each other, danced closely and kissed softly at different points throughout the night.

"This place is fire. I'm so glad we decided to come here Babe." They took a break from dancing and sat down, but Taryn kept moving her shoulders back and forth to the fast-paced beat of the Cuban music.

"Yes! It's exactly what I thought it would be. Babe, you are wearing that red dress, and those shoes are setting it off. Perfect for tonight."

"Was it worth the wait?" Taryn stared at Aman and gave him that million-dollar smile that he had told her so many times he completely loved.

"Yes, ma'am! It was more than worth it." Aman gave Taryn a seductive look that signaled that he wanted to make love to her.

"I've taken care of the check. Are you ready to go?" Taryn was hot and bothered and she wanted to make love to Aman, too.

"Thank you. I really appreciate you for tonight. I'm so ready." Aman got up and walked over to Taryn to pull out her chair.

As she stood up, he grabbed her from behind and kissed the back of her neck. They walked out of the restaurant with her arm around his waist and his arm around her shoulders. On the ride home, they decided Taryn would go to Aman's house since they met at the restaurant after work and drove separate cars. Taryn called Damon on the way to Aman's house to let him know she wasn't coming home.

"Hey Mom."

"Hey, Sweetie! Did I wake you?"

"Yeah, I was knocked out."

"Sorry, just wanted to let you know that Aman and I just finished dinner and dancing. It's late so I'm going to stay at his house tonight instead of driving all the way home. Everything okay with you?"

"I'm good. I was wondering where you were. You sound like you had fun tonight."

"I did! It's been a while since I've had this much fun.

"I'm glad. You deserve it. I'm going back to sleep. Enjoy your evening and I'll see you tomorrow after I get out of school."

"Ok, Babe. Sleep tight and sweet dreams." Taryn ended the call with Damon as she pulled into Aman's driveway and parked her car in the open garage space next to his.

Aman waited for her and they entered his house together. They didn't waste any time getting to his bedroom as they both knew exactly what they wanted.

"I've been waiting for this all day." Aman caressed Taryn's body in all the ways she liked as he unzipped her dress.

"Taryn wrapped her arms around his neck and pulled him close to kiss him deeply, and they explored each other with their tongues as they made their way to his queen-sized plush bed.

Aman stopped for a moment to light a candle and turn on music. Lauren Hill and Bob Marley's *Turn Your Lights Down Low* was playing as the two made sweet love. The smell of vanilla and lavender filled the air and stimulated all their senses.

During their love making, Aman told Taryn that one thing that every woman wanted to hear in a moment of passion but may question later after that moment is over.

"I love you, Taryn Madrid." Aman kissed Taryn again and again.

"I love you too, Aman Eniale." Taryn kissed him back.

They slept in each other's arms into the morning. They both had to go to work the next day so there wasn't time for a lot of deep conversation. Taryn didn't forget what Aman had said about loving her. She decided later that day to bring it up.

"Last night you told me you love me. You remember that?" Taryn asked Aman about what he had said as she was riding home from work.

"Yes, of course I remember. I do love you. I didn't expect to fall for you so soon. I didn't expect for someone like you to come into my life." Aman was honest and vulnerable.

"You said it, too. Did you mean it?" Aman asked Taryn the same question.

"Yes, I did. I've been feeling it for a while now. It's so crazy because I wasn't looking for anything and it's been so nice having someone to enjoy life with. I didn't have any expectations for our relationship when we started except that we would treat each other well and take care to build our friendship. This just kinda happened." Taryn was honest with him.

"Well, no pressure. Let's just see where this love thing takes us. Deal?" Aman was being mature about it.

"It's a deal, my friend. Now…about last night." They both laughed as they relived the moments with one another sharing how much they enjoyed each part of the night.

Taryn and Aman dated for two years and got to know one another in every way. They spent time together having lunch dates, dinner dates, traveling together and enjoying their family and friends together. Their relationship blossomed as Taryn now had new skills that she used to create a thriving relationship with Aman. One night at dinner, Taryn decided to have a talk with Aman about making plans for the future.

"I believe our relationship is worth investing in long term. I think we should think about moving to the next level. We have a great relationship built on friendship, love, truth, honesty and commitment. I see a future for us." Taryn knew how to express herself and she wanted to see where Aman was.

"Taryn, you know I love you. What more do you need?"

"I want it all and everything that comes with it."

"You have it all. You have my heart. I love you."

Aman would never really discuss a committed future with Taryn. Every time she brought it up, he seemed to listen, but he didn't say much else, or he would quickly change the subject.

One day out of frustration, she called Socar because she knew something was off with him. She also knew that time would tell her everything she needed to know. She didn't worry about it, but she did begin to pay more attention to his actions.

"Being in relationship with Aman is like a riddle, a clue and a joke all at the same time." Taryn laughed with Socar over the phone, except she wasn't laughing inside.

"Taryn, sometimes you just have to have patience with people. Let God transform your heart through this relationship. Sometimes it's not about the other person. Sometimes it's all about you." Taryn knew that what Socar said made sense and that she was definitely being transformed through her relationship with Aman.

The last thing she wanted to do was rush into a serious commitment and end up in a bad situation with someone who wasn't capable or ready to commit. That had been a disaster in her previous marriage to Ryan and she definitely wasn't doing that again.

CHAPTER 11

Learning the Truth

"And ye shall know the truth, and the truth shall make you free." John 8:32 (KJV)

A man had been hiding a big secret from Taryn - one that could destroy their relationship when she learned the truth. It was just a matter of time. It proved to be a painful truth and neither Taryn nor Aman were prepared for the truth to come out so unexpectedly that early September morning.

It had been a rough week at work for Taryn. She was under a lot of stress trying to find a viable solution for the McCoy commercial deal that wouldn't require her to take a huge reduction in her commission, like the Abdullah deal required earlier in her career. She also had to make sure not to leave room for a competitor to make a better offer. Over the years, Taryn had become quite comfortable in the commercial real estate world. She was no longer a rookie and had closed numerous deals. Now that she had made her mark, the competition had become even more fierce. There was a lot of money to be made and it could be cutthroat at times. It was just the kind of game Taryn liked to play. It challenged her to maintain her integrity and character in the midst of snakes and vultures. Her strategy was solid. She would build strong, trusting relationships with her clients to learn about what they really cared about. She would use that information to think strategically and become creative in solving their problems. She had learned what pitfalls to avoid and there were many when closing these deals.

Every time she had a closing coming up, she would have trouble sleeping the night before the closing. To boot, Taryn had been tossing and turning all night trying not to think of what could go wrong. She was anxious about the final closing meeting that morning with Mr. McCoy, the client. As she was lying in bed, she anticipated another long day at the office with lots of meetings. She was having her morning prayer time with God about her day when her phone rang. It was Aman.

"Good morning, Babe! How are you?" Aman said in his usual happy morning voice.

"I'm good! How are you?" Taryn got up and headed to the bathroom to get ready for work. She put the phone on speaker and grabbed a washcloth to wash her face.

"You have your big deal today. Are you ready?" Aman always supported Taryn's work.

"Yeah, I'm still working on it, but I think I can figure it out. I'm definitely ready to get this over with." Taryn slightly chuckled.

"Hey Babe! Let me call you back in a minute," Aman quickly interjected before they could fully discuss their workday and make plans for the weekend.

"Sure! No problem Honey." Taryn expected Aman to end the call, but he didn't. She was across the room away from her phone busy styling her hair and doing her makeup. She needed to cover the dark circles from her sleepless night.

She heard his footsteps as he walked away from his phone into the next room. Aman lived in an older house and his wood floors squeaked whenever he moved from room to room. His walls were paper thin, and you could hear right through them. Taryn could hear him talking in the next room. She continued putting on her makeup but noticed that Aman seemed to be having a conversation with someone. She walked over to the phone to hang it up but decided to listen instead.

"Good morning, son!" Taryn heard Aman say to someone after she heard the familiar sound that his computer made whenever he made a Facetime call.

Taryn and Aman had used Facetime to talk many times before when either of them was away on business trips. She knew the sound and she knew he was at home alone. At least she thought he was.

"He must be on his computer on Facetime. Wait a minute, did he say 'son'?" Taryn put her hand over her mouth. Her eyes bulged and eyebrows creased as she picked up her phone. She took her phone off the speaker and put it up to her ear being sure to mute the phone so Aman wouldn't hear her. She wanted to be sure she could better hear all of the conversation.

"Hi Daddy!" Taryn clearly heard a little voice speaking back to Aman.

"Oh my God! He has a son?" Taryn mouthed as she watched herself in the bathroom mirror shaking her head in disbelief.

Her heart was racing. She knew Aman had been hiding something, but never in a million years would she have imagined that there was a child involved. She knew about his teenage daughter, but a son!

"Daddy, are you coming to see me this weekend?" Aman's son asked in his little voice. Taryn was completely heartbroken as the child sounded so cute and innocent. She pictured an adorable little boy, maybe five years old. Taryn loved little children.

"Yes, I am. You know I'll be there on Sunday, just like always, son." Aman reassured the little boy. He always had a good reason for why he couldn't spend time with Taryn on Sunday. He would say he was studying on Sunday, or he had to prepare for the work week. The truth was, he was going to see his son. Where was his son? Who was the child's mother? Taryn had so many questions. She kept her ear pressed to the phone hoping to get answers to her unasked questions.

"Let me talk to your mommy now. You have a great day at school, lil man. Be good and I'll see you Sunday. Daddy loves you, son." Aman ended the conversation with his son.

"I love you too Daddy!"

"Hey, how are you?" Aman cordially asked the woman who must have appeared on the screen after the child.

"Look, I don't have time for a whole lot of faking like you're concerned about me this morning." From what Taryn could hear, the woman seemed angry and she spoke with a no-nonsense tone to Aman.

Taryn pressed her ear to the phone even harder and she turned up her volume to make sure she could hear every word spoken.

"Did you deposit the money?" The woman got right to the point.

"Yes, I did. I'm coming to get him on Sunday. Is that alright?" Aman changed his tone of voice to business to match hers.

"Yes, that's fine. We will be here. Can you get here before nine? I have church and I don't want to be late. If you are not here when I get ready to leave, you will have to get him from the church, or you will have to wait until we get out." The woman gave Aman explicit instructions and Taryn knew exactly why. Aman had a habit of being late for everything.

"I will be there. And...I will be there before nine." Aman laughed as he knew being late was his signature. He couldn't deny it to anyone who knew him. Apparently, this woman knew him well. Taryn's top lip flickered. There was someone else who knew Aman like she did.

Aman and the woman said goodbye before Aman came back into the room and grabbed his phone. Taryn was still listening. She was in shock.

"Hello?" Aman realized he hadn't ended the call with Taryn. He reluctantly spoke into his phone praying he hadn't made the mistake that he soon realized he had.

"Did I just hear what I thought I heard?" Taryn sat down on the edge of her bed and held her forehead as if she would pass out. Her voice trembled in defeat as she spoke to Aman.

There was a long pause before Aman finally answered.

"Yes, Taryn, I have a son." Aman sighed deeply as he knew it was time to come clean. He paused for a long time before answering Taryn. He hung his head as he quietly whispered the words that confirmed what Taryn wished she hadn't heard.

"I didn't want to tell you because I knew you would be angry," Aman continued, "I'm sorry, Taryn. I don't know what

I was thinking." Aman was hoping Taryn wouldn't hang up on him.

"You shouldn't have done that Aman! You should've told me." Taryn was incensed and screamed loudly at him through the phone.

"I know. You're right. I should've." Aman conceded.

When? How? Taryn was completely confused and at a loss for words that made sense because what she was trying to process made absolutely no sense to her.

"I'm sorry Taryn." Aman whispered.

"Why would you do this? Who does this, Aman? Taryn shifted off the bed and paced back and forth. Her arms were flying in the air. She wanted to punch Aman for disrespecting their relationship and crossing all kinds of lines without her consent.

It made Taryn physically sick. She ran to the bathroom and leaned over the sink facing the truth that Aman was a liar, a cheater and worse than that, a father to a child she didn't even know existed until now. Had she not listened in on the call she still wouldn't have known about his son.

"When were you going to tell me Aman?" She screamed after spitting out the foam that had risen from her belly into her throat. "This is completely crazy to me. You know I can't stand a liar. I'm seriously sick to my stomach right now." Taryn was yelling like a crazed mad woman through the phone.

"Taryn, I have no words to explain this. I didn't want to lose you. You're right, I know. I just didn't know how to tell you that I screwed up. I didn't want to lose you. I'm so sorry." After dumping everything on Taryn in one breath, Aman went silent.

"You had no right to do this. How could you keep this from me? You must be crazy, Aman. Or maybe I'm crazy." Taryn put her hand to her forehead. She was heated as she walked back into her room to sit down.

"You're not crazy, Taryn. It's me. Please don't take any blame for this. This is all me. I have some really serious issues that I need to deal with. I'm so sorry." Aman confessed his lies and his deceit.

"How old is your son, Aman?" Taryn wanted to know details as she was trying to put the puzzle pieces together.

"He's four," Aman reluctantly responded to Taryn's question. He never liked to be questioned but if he didn't answer Taryn right then, she would end the conversation and never talk to him again.

"Oh my God, Aman! You've had this child since you and I have been together? I can't believe this." Taryn did the math. They had been dating for almost five years, and when she realized he had cheated on her and that he had been deceitful all the years of their relationship, she rushed toward the bathroom again wanting to vomit.

"Taryn, I'm so sorry. I wanted to tell you so many times. I just didn't know how. I messed up. I didn't want to lose you. Taryn, I love you! I'm so sorry, baby." Aman sounded sincere, but Taryn couldn't forget that he didn't come clean about all of this on his own.

He had kept this secret for at least four years so who knows how long he had carried on the relationship with the child's mother. Taryn would've respected him more if he had come clean on his own instead of her finding out about it haphazardly. It was going to be painful either way. But at least if he had offered the information on his own, she could've felt like he was taking responsibility for his actions, which could signal a realization that he needed to make some drastic changes in his character.

"Aman, you don't love me. You love yourself. You have always been a selfish…" Taryn stopped herself before she called him outside his name. "You had no plans of telling me anything. What else have you kept from me? What else don't I know about you? Who are you?" Taryn was shaking her head slowly back and forth.

Taryn held on to the counter in the bathroom praying this nightmare would end.

"All the times I questioned where you were over these years." Aman had been unavailable. "There were so many times when I questioned myself for trying to be supportive of you. I fought really hard not to let all the scars from my relationship with Ryan come into my relationship with you, Aman. I got it all wrong once again. Clearly, I have been too supportive of you. I didn't question you enough when I should have been firm about getting answers about your whereabouts and your finances." Taryn talked to Aman while looking at herself in the bathroom mirror.

"Who is she?" Taryn asked Aman about the woman on the phone as she now turned her attention away from the child to the mother.

"Someone I used to be in a relationship with before you and I began dating." Aman was vague on purpose. That was his slick way of keeping his lies and deceitfulness going. He had a way of omitting important information because he just didn't say very much about things that he wanted to keep private.

"What is her name, Aman?" Taryn asked him more directly. "And just stop already with the mysterious act." She was more annoyed that he was still trying to play games with her.

"Her name is Shelia. We used to date. When you and I first met, we were ending our relationship, but we weren't done yet. I went back a few times, but I have not been with her since our son was born. I don't want her. I don't love her. We are parents to our son and that's it. I'm sorry, Taryn." Aman was forthcoming with the information, but Taryn didn't believe anything he said because this new information had shaken the very foundation of any trust that they had built in their relationship.

"As many times as you've said, 'I'm sorry,' you are absolutely right. You are sorry!" Taryn no longer felt sick to her stomach. All she felt now was pure disgust. "I don't believe you. I don't trust you. You know what...I need a minute. I need time to figure all this out. I can't continue to talk about this right now. I have to go to work." Taryn was ready to end the call.

"I understand if you don't ever want to talk to me again. I deserve that. I just want you to know it's not you. It's all me. I'm so sorry." Aman rushed to say that before Taryn could hang up.

Taryn ended the call and looked in the mirror. Her eyes were bulging and red. So much for all the work she had put into her makeup that morning. She felt like she needed to have a good cry, but she didn't have time. She had a meeting in less than two hours and a full day of meetings after that. She wanted to cancel everything, crawl into bed and go back to sleep. If this had been a bad dream she could go back to sleep, wake up, and it would be a new day. She wanted to undo the last thirty minutes of her life. No such luck. She had to press on and get through the day.

The funny thing was, God had prepared her for this. She had prayed and asked God to reveal to her what was going on with Aman. She knew something wasn't right with him and she asked God to show her. Taryn knew that God was faithful, and it would eventually be revealed when she was ready. Unfortunately for her, she wasn't ready that morning.

CHAPTER 12

Start with Forgiveness

"Be kind to one another, tenderhearted, forgiving one another, as God in Christ forgave you." Ephesians 4:32 (ESV)

Taryn rode to work in complete silence making her way through the rush hour traffic. She didn't realize she was at work until she pulled into the parking garage and Dreya appeared at her car door. The rest of the trip was a blur.

"Good morning!" Dreya was impeccably dressed wearing a black dress and stilettos.

"Good morning!" Taryn grabbed her purse and computer bag from the seat and got out of the car.

"I know you have the meeting this morning and I wanted to wish you good luck today." Dreya was enthusiastic.

"Thank you, I may need it." Taryn shook her head back and forth.

"You got this, sis!" Dreya was clueless about what Taryn had just experienced at home and Taryn couldn't tell her.

"Can you do a celebratory lunch today?" Dreya walked ahead of Taryn.

"Let me see how the morning goes and I can let you know. I'll have my assistant call you if I can." Dreya pressed the elevator button to take them to their office.

"Ok, sounds good, I'll see you later. Go get 'em!" Dreya got off the elevator first and disappeared into her office.

"Thanks, friend!" Taryn followed and walked toward her assistant who was standing near her office chatting with another assistant.

"Good morning Ms. Madrid!" Taryn's assistant followed her into her office.

"Good morning, how are you? Are the documents ready for the meeting?" Taryn got right down to business.

"Yes ma'am. They're right there. That should answer all their questions. I ran the numbers, and everything is in order. You're taking a big hit in your commission and I hope they appreciate the sacrifice you're making to pull this off." She reminded Taryn what she was giving up.

"Yeah, I've been doing this for a while. You win some and you lose some. You always keep learning along the way. I'll make it up on the next deal." Taryn sat in her chair to review the budget sheet one more time.

"That's why you're the commercial real estate expert." Lindsey pointed to Taryn.

Taryn laughed. "I receive that. Can you call me when they're ready? Please give me a minute and close the door. Thank you." Taryn looked at her phone that had been buzzing. There were several new texts from Aman.

She put the phone face down on her desk and gathered herself. A few minutes later her office phone rang; it was her assistant.

"They're ready for you," Lindsey said.

Taryn leaped out of her chair. "Thank you!" She walked confidently down the hall to the conference room where four men were waiting.

She entered the room and greeted everyone with a handshake.

"Gentlemen, thank you for being here so early this morning. I will have you out of here in just enough time to tee up." They all laughed.

"I know there have been some questions about the numbers, and I've reworked them. I think this will make everyone happy." Taryn handed them all a packet.

"Please turn your attention to page thirty-four in particular. There is where you will find the reworked numbers. I made you a counteroffer that you simply can't refuse." Taryn sat down and gave them time to review the information.

After two hours of intense discussion and volleying, the deal was done.

"You're right, Ms. Madrid, this is a deal we can all live with. We're ready to sign." One of the men chimed in.

"Excellent!" Taryn got up from the table and thanked the client.

"I can't wait to get started on this project and I look forward to working with all of you." Taryn shook each hand before leaving the room.

She stopped by Dreya's office.

"So, how did it go?" Dreya was smiling from ear to ear.

"It's done!" Taryn raised her hand to give Dreya a high five.

"I knew you could do it! Proud of you, sis." Dreya did a little dance.

"Now about that celebratory lunch." They both laughed.

Taryn kept ignoring Aman's attempts to reach out to her and he eventually got the message and stopped. She was relieved and she decided she wasn't going to deal with Aman's foolishness right then. She was going to deal with that later. Right then, she was going to celebrate closing one of the biggest deals of her career. She walked back to her office to share the good news with Lindsey.

"It's done! Everything went swimmingly! Thank you so much for your hard word to make me shine. You're the best!" She pointed at Lindsey.

"My pleasure Ms. Madrid." Lindsey did a curtsey and they both laughed.

"Dreya and I are going to lunch. Let me buy you lunch. Order whatever you like and charge it to my account."

"Okay, thank you!" Lindsey left Taryn's office.

Taryn looked at her phone. Aman had left 14 text messages and she had 2 missed calls from him. Taryn shook her head and deleted the messages and cleared the missed calls from her phone. She dialed Dreya's office.

"Hey girl! I'm ready whenever you are."

"Let's do it. I'm starving."

"You always are. I don't know how you stay so thin."

"I know. So greedy." They both laughed.

Taryn and Dreya went to lunch and after lunch they did a little shopping. They decided they would make their celebration last for the rest of the workday. Taryn was floating on cloud nine the entire day and she shared with Dreya.

"It is such a good feeling to work hard and win with this deal." Taryn looked for her size in a blouse she liked.

"Girl, I can only imagine. I'm so happy for you. This is a game changer you know." Dreya was nearby thumbing through another rack looking for a skirt she liked.

"Yes, I know. So many doors opened today for me and the company."

"I admire your tenacity. Keep climbing to the top sis. I'm right behind you." They gave each other a high five.

They shopped a little more, grabbed ice cream for dessert and headed home.

When she got home that evening Damon was in the kitchen with one of his friends from high school drinking Gatorade and talking about last night's basketball game between the Lakers and Wizards. Damon was a huge Lakers fan and he loved Kobe Bryant. Taryn could hear them as she came in. They had just finished playing basketball in the driveway before she pulled up.

"Oh, hey Mom. You remember my friend." The young man introduced himself. They chatted a minute about school and he said he had to get home. Damon walked him out and came back into the kitchen.

"So, what's up with you? How was your day?" Damon seemed genuinely interested.

"I had a great day! Finally settled on a commercial deal I had been working on that seemed like it wasn't going to come through. I closed it today." Taryn held up her hand to get a high five from Damon.

"Awesome! Congratulations!" Damon returned his mom's high five.

"Thank you, Baby!" Taryn opened the refrigerator to get a bottle of water.

"Oh, I almost forgot to tell you...Mr. Aman came by here. I told him you weren't home yet. He seemed worried. Is everything okay?" Damon looked at Taryn for the answer.

Taryn shook her head. She hadn't thought about Aman for a minute, but Damon's question and the mention of his name reminded her of the mess he had created.

"No, everything is not okay. But it's nothing you need to be worried about. I'll figure it out." Taryn looked down at the floor.

"Aw man! I'm sorry. I hope it works out, Mom. You seem really happy with him. It's kinda the first time I've seen you happy in a while." Damon gave Taryn a hug.

"I don't know, son. There are some things you can't recover from." Taryn shook her head as she rested on Damon's chest.

"Well either way, I'm really proud of you. I've seen some good changes in you, and I know it wasn't easy to give love another try after you and Dad divorced." Damon gave Taryn an extra squeeze and she squeezed him back.

It felt good for Taryn to have Damon's arms around her. She needed that hug. Damon let Taryn know he was there for her and they watched a movie together that night. It took Taryn's mind off Aman for a few hours.

That night when she went to bed, she laid there thinking about what happened that morning. She was so angry she couldn't sleep. Taryn got up, turned on the light and decided to journal her feelings.

I found out Aman has a son this morning. I'm so pissed with him. I'm angry with myself. I can't believe I didn't know this man was capable of hiding such important information. Am I that desperate that I overlooked the obvious? There's something clearly wrong with my choice of men. I don't want to talk to him right now. He's been calling and texting me all day. I don't want to be mean and ugly, but that's how I'm feeling inside right now. I want to curse him out, but I know that won't solve anything. I feel so conflicted. I love him, but right now I hate him too. How could anyone be so careless with their relationships. How could I be involved with someone who could be so irresponsible? Every time I think about him now, all I think about is the little voice on the phone. This has changed everything. Things will never be the same between us again. I can't trust him ever again. It's going to be a long time before I can even talk to him again. Even though I miss him already. I wanted to share my good news with him today and then I remembered this morning. I just don't understand all of this, but I know I will one day. I feel so empty inside right now. Lord, please help me make it through this.

Taryn closed her journal, sat it on the table next to her bed and laid down. She closed her eyes and this time; she was able to fall asleep. Taryn would journal each night when she couldn't fall asleep because she was thinking about Aman. One night the journaling wasn't helping. She scrolled through her phone on social media and came to a YouTube video on forgiveness. She watched the video out of curiosity. It was an interview with Bishop T. D. Jakes, and he was sharing about who benefits when people choose to forgive. Taryn thought about Aman as she watched the video. After watching the video, she wrote in her journal.

What would it look like to forgive Aman? What would it take for me to forgive him?

A few weeks had passed, and Aman had stopped obsessively calling, texting and leaving apologetic voicemails. Taryn had not responded to any of his attempts to contact her. She knew she would have to talk to him at some point, but she didn't want to do it angry. It was a Saturday morning and Taryn had slept in. She had gone to bed early the night before and she was well rested enough to talk to Aman when he called out of nowhere that morning.

"Hello!" Taryn reluctantly held the phone up to her ear and sighed deeply as she sat up in her bed.

She listened to Aman go on and on for fifteen minutes about how sorry he was before she broke her silence. Forgiveness was definitely not the first thing Taryn wanted to give Aman, but it was on her mind and in her heart at that moment.

"I forgive you." She had been giving him the side eye through the phone, as she rolled over to her other side in her king-sized bed. She bit and twisted her lips for the entire fifteen minutes that he stumbled over his words trying to explain the unexplainable.

As she silently wept, she could hear Aman softly weeping through the phone. Taryn pulled the down comforter closer to her neck. The room had become cold.

"I don't know what to say, Taryn. Thank you! I know I don't deserve your forgiveness, but I'm grateful for it." Aman was surprised and unsure of what to say next. They sat in silence on the phone listening to each other sniff as they both sobbed. Then Taryn hung up without saying another word.

Over those two weeks, Taryn had also taken some time to process the information with Socar. She was in a better space than the weeks before when she struggled to hear anything through the anger, disappointment and betrayal she felt. She and Socar spent time discussing over the phone and meeting face to face to uncover the truth. They prayed and reflected on Aman's behavior and on Taryn's own behavior. Socar helped her be honest. It was hard, but it was very necessary for her to move forward. Taryn had been saying, probably from the beginning of their relationship, that there was something Aman was hiding. It was almost a relief for her that the actual truth had come out and she could finally confront it with Socar's support. The two had a phone conversation.

"I'm not surprised by any of what you are sharing with me about Aman's infidelity and lies. I was able to see that Aman had some character flaws from the moment I first met him." Socar chewed the food she had stuffed in her mouth and smacked in Taryn's ear.

"Really! Why didn't you tell me?" Taryn wrinkled her brow and held the phone from her ear to look at it.

"Come on, Taryn, you can't be that naïve, can you? I don't always want to have to tell you everything. Some things you have to figure out on your own. His conversation was shallow, and he has an ego the size of a mountain." Socar almost yelled at Taryn for being so thick headed.

"I mean, I knew he had some deep insecurities," Taryn whispered.

"Yeah, the kind of deep insecurities that you and no other woman would ever be able to love him enough through. He would have to do that work on himself to fix whatever is ailing him." Socar slapped Taryn upside the head with her words to knock some sense into her.

"You know Socar...I realize that Aman was too caught up in trying to look like a gentleman instead of actually being a gentleman. I saw right through his façade too, and I knew it was just a matter of time before I would learn the truth." Taryn admitted she was waiting for the other shoe to drop on Aman.

"That kind of man will always need his ego stroked by someone else other than one woman. I didn't say anything because I knew you weren't ready to hear it nor address it, even though I could clearly see it in Aman." Socar was softer in her tone this time.

"Why do people lie?" They were sitting in the living room filled with hundreds of books and interesting trinkets from Socar's many excursions around the world.

Taryn had been smiling, which was a welcome change from the weeks before when Socar had to comfort her during bouts of sobbing. Taryn had made emotional progress and she was able to talk without crying. Taryn stared at an African painting in Socar's living room. For her, the painting represented the strength and beauty of the African people. She waited for Socar to say something profound in response to her unanswerable question.

"Sweetie, we're just human beings. From the beginning of time, people have lied." Socar reached across the sofa and grabbed Taryn's hand as she offered her the simplest most honest answer she could muster at the time. Taryn let out a big sigh.

"All I know is when people lie and we find out about it, we have a choice. We can respond with compassion, understanding, forgiveness and love because that is what Christ does for us daily. There is no other way." Socar laughed a hearty laugh as she had reminded Taryn of this truth on more than one occasion and it was usually when Taryn was most reluctant to hear it. But Socar was right.

Taryn had tried to feel sorry for herself, but Socar wouldn't let her become comfortable wallowing in self-pity. She wouldn't let her play the victim. Taryn wasn't a victim. She was just as much responsible for her part in supporting Aman's behavior and his ability to lie and keep secrets. Socar had helped Taryn discover her part in the foolishness.

"I know I'm not a victim. I have to own my part in this. I know that now. I knew there was something wrong and I ignored it. Why?" Taryn raised her hands palms up in front of her as she sat across the kitchen table from Socar and looked her in the eye. Her palms up represented an act of surrender for Taryn. She was ready to surrender to the truth of why she chose to ignore all the signs that told her something was going on with Aman.

They had moved to the kitchen to have lunch. Socar had made her famous crab cakes. Taryn loved them. As they prepared to eat lunch, Socar reinforced Taryn's part in the mess.

"You're right. You're not a victim. Your 'why' is the question you have to answer. Why did you overlook the obvious? And you must answer it today, and you must keep on answering it, so it doesn't happen again." Socar had been careful with Taryn in those few weeks. She didn't push too hard, but she wanted Taryn to see her blind spots in this relationship. She was also preparing Taryn for the future.

Taryn gained a new understanding about the part that she played in the whole situation. She had made the first phone call to Aman that started their relationship. She invited Aman into her bedroom before marriage and before really getting to know him. Their relationship had started based on lust and untruth. She had fed her flesh throughout the relationship because she was hungry and thirsty for love after having to rebuild her self-esteem from the divorce. She had to own that truth and it was an ugly truth. She had prayed about Aman before they started dating. God had given Taryn the recipe for the relationship and she chose not to follow it. She had to admit that to herself and to God. Had she turned back and listened to God's instructions at any point, things may have turned out differently.

When Taryn prayed about the relationship, God had given her the following instructions, "Seek Me first. Pray for one another. Worship together. And get your flesh under control. And I will bless you both abundantly."

At the time, God's message wasn't fully clear, so she didn't pay attention to it when she should've. Now that the truth had come out, was there too much destruction associated with it all? Should she just let it go? Should she let go of her desire to be with Aman and move on? There could be something new and beautiful waiting for her on her next level as she walked through the open door of her heart.

After much soul searching about her relationship with Aman, Taryn shared a story with Socar. "The truth I also have to face is that I had a moment of weakness within the first year of my relationship with Aman. I had packed the incident far away from my mind as I was embarrassed about it. Now that I've been reflecting and searching for how to move forward, somehow it came back to me. So, I understand how Aman could've gotten caught up with his child's mother when I confess to you my moment of weakness." Taryn looked away from Socar.

Socar stopped eating for a minute to give Taryn her full attention. "Really! Do tell what happened..."

"It happened about six months after Aman and I started dating. Aman was away for the weekend, like he was a lot of the time. It was a beautiful summer Saturday evening and I wanted to do something fun. An old friend, Ross Waldorf, from college had contacted me that morning and asked me to meet him for dinner. Ross and I had a brief fling when we were in college. It was nothing serious and we had kept in touch on social media over the years.

"Through our social media connection, I was aware that Ross had recently gone through a divorce and had three kids. I could relate and I sympathized with him being a new divorcee. I wanted to see how he was handling being single again. His invite came at the perfect time since I didn't have plans for the evening."

"Hey Taryn, it's been a long time. I am in town on business and I'd like to see you while I'm here. Are you free this evening?" Ross sent me a text message that morning.

"I innocently agreed to go out to dinner with him never intending for the evening to end with us being intimate with each other in any way.

Upon arriving at the five-star restaurant where we agreed to meet, I saw him from across the room and quickly wiped the drool from my lips. I was thinking, 'Wow! He looks really great. He looks much better than he does on social media.'

"He was wearing all black and his pecks and biceps were bulging through the short sleeve linen shirt. He always worked out even when we were in college. He lived in the gym.

"When I reached him and we embraced, I muttered into his chest, 'And he smells even better.' My whole upper body sank into his chest.

"I knew there was potential for things to turn flirtatious with Ross, but I was in control. I didn't want to become a rebound case because divorce had an emotional impact and it would take a while to sort through it all. I proceeded with caution being careful to avoid any risqué conversation with Ross.

"We had a wonderful dinner talking and catching up on old times. It was as if no time had passed since the last time we had seen each other. He ordered the surf and turf and I ordered the salmon. We both ordered a few drinks. The evening was perfect as we dined on the patio of the restaurant that sat on the Potomac River. The moonlight danced on the water and, every now and then, the soft breeze blew the smell of his cologne my way. We laughed so hard reminiscing about our days in college and it felt good to be out enjoying Ross' company."

"I'm sure it did, honey. It's nice to know you still got it even when you have a man," Socar laughed.

"You're a mess. You know that, right?" Taryn joined in with Socar's laughter.

"Anyway, Aman called a few times that evening. I ignored his calls. We were still getting to know one another, and I wasn't sure if our relationship was going anywhere. At the end of the evening, neither us wanted our time to end right then so we decided to find somewhere else to go dancing."

"Where are you staying?" Taryn asked to determine where they would go next.

"I'm at the Carlisle downtown. It's not too far from here." Ross pointed in the direction where he believed his hotel was.

"Ok! They actually have a really great club there with the best DJ in town on Saturday night. Are you in the mood for a little dancing?" Taryn started dancing and circling around Ross.

He grabbed her by the hand and joined in. "I sure am. Lead the way, lady!" Ross escorted Taryn to her car, and they drove separately to his hotel which was only a few miles away.

"Ross remembered that I love to dance, and I love music. I had been to the club a few times with Dreya, so I knew it would be a great spot for us to hit the dance floor and work off our food. We could hear the music before we even entered the club and just as I said, it was definitely the place to be on a Saturday night. The DJ was playing a nice mix of Go-go music, Reggae, Hip Hop, House and old school R&B. We hit the dance floor immediately and didn't come off until the lights came on indicating the club was about to close. We both agreed it had been a long time since we had enjoyed ourselves like that. We both needed that fun night. It was late and Ross refused to let me drive home."

"Why don't you just stay the night? I have a suite. I will sleep on the couch. I don't want you to drive home. It's too late." Ross had always looked out for me. He had always been protective of me, even when we were in college.

"I trusted Ross. I have known him for more than twenty years. I was exhausted as it was the early hours of the morning. Aman didn't usually call when he was away for the weekend, which should've been another sign for me. So, I agreed to sleep over."

"Okay, I agree. I'm very tired and I don't feel like driving home." We headed toward his hotel suite laughing and dancing all the way there.

Once we reached his suite, we continued to chat about old times as we sat on the living room sofa. There was a moment where Ross got serious.

"What did happen between me and you, Taryn? I mean, I really liked you back in college." Ross looked Taryn in the eye this time and he didn't turn away, but he propped his head up on his arm that was resting on the back of the couch.

"Are you kidding me? Who knows? I don't remember what was going on back then. We were young. We were carefree. Anything could've happened. Besides, you were funny looking back then." They both broke out into a belly laugh and it ended with them holding each other.

"I remember we always used to laugh like this. We had some good times." Ross pulled Taryn close and she didn't stop him.

"I agree. We did have some great times." Taryn snuggled up close to Ross and he kissed the back of her neck.

"We kissed one another deeply as we embraced. We shared sweet and tender kisses and soft touches as we both released our apprehension, let down our guard and settled into the moment. We caressed and held one another all night but we didn't make love because neither of us had protection. By how hot and bothered we each had become, it was clear we both definitely wanted to. We cuddled and slept late into mid-morning.

"I was so embarrassed that it happened. I could never tell Aman about it. He wouldn't understand, and I knew it would never happen again. It never did."

"So, you're human. You were then and you are now." Socar reassured her.

"Yes. I didn't really want to be with Ross that night. I just had a moment of weakness. Now I can understand how it could happen to Aman. I also understand what I needed to do to avoid it ever happening again. Even though Ross had tried to reach out to me several times when he was in town, I cut off all communication once I decided I wanted to be with Aman." Taryn stood up to refill her empty glass with lemonade.

Socar started eating again. "Thank you for sharing that with me. I know it wasn't easy for you."

"No, it wasn't. When Aman returned from his weekend away, he seemed distant from me. I had my own feelings of guilt for having been with Ross in such an intimate way. I noticed something different about Aman, but I ignored it because I was dealing with my own shame."

"Really, what was different about Aman?" Socar probed Taryn for more information.

"This might be TMI but since I'm already out here…I might as well say it." Taryn laughed a little.

"Go ahead." Socar confirmed she was listening.

"Well usually when Aman came home from a trip, he would desire intimacy with me. He would come over to my house as soon as his plane landed or if he drove, he would head straight to my house once he was back in town. But this time was different. It was days before he came over and when we did see one another, he barely embraced me. Of course, I was looking around trying to make sure he couldn't sense something was different about me because of the whole Ross incident. He was staring off into space and not listening to anything I was saying as if he was still a thousand miles away even though I was there right in front of him."

"How did that make you feel?" Socar put her empty plate in the sink in the kitchen.

"I remember feeling completely rejected by Aman during that time. The reality was that Aman had been having an ongoing rendezvous of his own with the mother of his child. Once I did the math, that weekend was around the time that Aman probably found out that Shelia was pregnant with their son. It makes me sick to think of it." Taryn rubbed her stomach.

"Yeah, that's got to be really hard. You're doing okay though. You will get through this." Socar reassured her.

"Yeah, I know I will. The worst part of all of it is the rejection that cuts deeply within my spirit. Aman told me he didn't want to have any more children. I accepted it, even though there was a lingering desire to still have another child. I had waited and now that Damon was getting ready to go to college, I didn't want to start over with raising a child. Not to mention, he and I aren't married. I couldn't see myself as a single mother again. For him to go and create a whole child with another person physically hurts like a knife being thrust into my body."

"I can only imagine." Socar was shaking her head back and forth as she sucked her teeth to get a piece of food out.

"All the times I decided to remain faithful to Aman except for that one night with Ross. I have to be honest, in these last few weeks, I've wanted to pick up the phone and call Ross and finish what we started that night. I wanted Aman to hurt like I was hurting. I knew that wouldn't be fair to Ross nor was that the answer. I know I had to forgive Aman, but I don't know if I can move past these overwhelming feelings of rejection that have nearly crippled me for the weeks since uncovering his devastating secret."

CHAPTER **13**

Rejecting Rejection

"As you come to him, the living Stone - rejected by men but chosen by God and precious to him." I Peter 2:4 (NIV)

Taryn had to deal with feelings of rejection once she found out Aman had been with another woman and had conceived a child as a result of it. She also understood it for what it was. At the end of the day, none of what Aman decided to do by carrying on this relationship and hiding his child was about her. Aman's deceitfulness and infidelity were all about him. It was all about his selfishness, his immaturity, his lack of loyalty, honesty and integrity. She was clear about this. But it still hurt like a fresh open wound. She was more than enough woman for Aman or any man, but his behavior made her jealous and envious. It was something she never liked to confront because it chipped away at her value and self-worth.

"People don't have the ability to do anything to you unless you allow it." Taryn could hear Grandma Bella's voice echoing in her head as she read a journal entry she had written.

She wished she could've picked up the phone and called Grandma Bella at that moment. Taryn was sure she would've had the right answer for this situation with Aman. If Taryn chose to stay in Aman's life, she would have to deal with the child and his mother. It would be a constant reminder of Aman's infidelity for as long as they were together.

"I can't believe he's the father of a four-year-old child." Taryn spoke to the mirror, shook her head as she looked in the mirror at the dark circles that had taken residency under her eyes. She had been repeating it over and over, as if saying it multiple times would somehow change it.

The reality of it changed the whole way she perceived Aman. It changed everything about their relationship. In a single moment, she went from dating a man who she believed had only one young adult daughter to discovering he was a father of two children, one of which was a young son. The rules were different for their relationship now. Aman's child would always come first, as he always should. Taryn just resented the fact that Aman didn't tell her back when he first found out about Shelia's pregnancy. Their relationship was still fairly new and if given the choice, she may have decided to end their relationship. At that time, she wasn't as emotionally involved as she had become over the last five years.

When Aman called her again, Taryn was better prepared to talk with him, but she was still hurt. "I may have made a different choice for myself had I known the truth. I feel like the decision was made for me and my choice was stolen away." Taryn seethed even more with anger and she could feel bitterness starting to set in as she spoke to Aman through the phone.

"Taryn, this is probably the thousandth conversation we've had about this in the last few months. I don't know what else to say, but I'm sorry." Aman was sympathetic to Taryn's need to go over and over everything that happened again and again. If he displayed anything but patience, he would lose Taryn for good.

Taryn listened to Aman as she bounced her neck from side to side like an athlete preparing for a game. She needed to release the stress coursing through her body.

"I can't change what's already happened. Trust me, if I could, I would. I can only tell you that I know I love you. I want to be with you. And I'm sorry for all the pain I've caused you." Aman responded every time with the same lines as if he had rehearsed them from a script.

Taryn had done a lot of soul searching and concluded that she had a choice now. She could choose to continue in the relationship with Aman, but she wasn't sure if she would, given Aman had been so irresponsible with his child and with her. Aman had committed to try to do everything he could to make it work, even though Taryn didn't make him any promises. She made it clear she wasn't sure she could carry on given so much had happened. At best, they would need to start over with rebuilding their friendship around the new circumstances before trying to have a relationship.

They had decided to meet since another full month had passed since they had seen each other face-to-face, and Taryn could finally stomach the sight of Aman again. It was weird to be sitting across the table talking to him. He seemed like a familiar stranger. It was as if she knew him, but given the new information, she didn't know Aman at all.

"Help me understand what you were thinking by hiding your son all these years. I just don't understand it, and I'm trying really hard." Taryn looked Aman in the eyes as she sat across from him at the dinner table of one of their favorite restaurants.

"I don't know what I was thinking. I wasn't thinking. I was living in fear. I was afraid of you finding out." Aman hurried his words. "I was afraid of losing you. I was just afraid of everything. For the first time in a long time, I haven't been afraid. I'm not afraid anymore. The worst has already happened and I'm learning to be at peace with it. I'm learning to own my mistakes, my failures and all of my disappointments." Aman spoke from his heart. Taryn could see that his mood seemed lighter and he was definitely more consistent than he probably had ever been in their entire relationship. "You finding out about my son has made me a different person. I've had a breakthrough. Throughout our relationship, there were times when I would be lost in worry. I was always worried about you finding out. You had to notice it."

"Yes, I did." Taryn sipped ice water.

It wasn't a good place. Fear is never a good place. I would try to relax and enjoy our time together whether we were having dinner or enjoying a movie, and something would trigger a memory or a thought of my son and feelings of regret would come over me."

"Yes, I've seen that look before...too many times." Taryn rolled her eyes. Your brow would wrinkle, and your face would contort indicating you were in that bad head space again. It bothered me."

"Yeah, and when you brought it to my attention, and you did every time, I would say it was nothing. I would immediately fix my face and change the subject."

"I knew something was bothering you. I just couldn't put my finger on it."

"It had absolutely nothing to do with you. It was all about the secret I was hiding." It wasn't your job to make me move beyond my fear. It was clearly something I had to work through on my own."

Taryn and Aman finished talking through dinner. Once Taryn got settled at home after dinner, she sat down to write in her journal…

Since I learned the truth, I have these overwhelming feelings of rejection. Learning that Aman had a child with another woman is so devastating because I wanted to be in every part of Aman's world. He never really let me in all the way. I understand why now. Now that I know the truth, I can finally deal with how powerful the feelings of rejection are for me. Even though I knew Aman was hiding something and that's why he wouldn't let me all the way in, I still tried to make it work to avoid dealing with the reality of rejection. Rejection hurts. It tells me I'm not good enough. It says Aman chose someone else over me. It screams at me and tells me I'm not what Aman wants. It is so painful for me to experience rejection, and I have to admit I have allowed the years to pass without addressing my feelings that there was something that Aman was hiding. I have to admit that I didn't want to lose him. I have to face that I was also living in fear too. This fear of rejection has left me feeling somewhat powerless in my relationship with Aman.

Now that I better understand what was motivating me and driving my relationship with Aman, I can begin to explore the other side of rejection from a different perspective. I have learned from Socar that it is always all about perspective. If I take a glass-half-full perspective, I know on the opposite side of rejection awaits opportunity. There is a new opportunity for me and Aman to rebuild a friendship and potentially a relationship, if we choose to do the work to make it happen. There is also now the opportunity for someone new to come into my life that is more of a match for what I truly desire if that is what I choose. I realize I can't make Aman see what he can't see.

Taryn put her journal down and picked up the phone to call Socar. They had started checking in every evening as Taryn continued to heal from the experience with Aman. Socar was a true accountability partner, and Taryn was blessed to have her.

"When rejection occurs, it can close one door, but it also pushes the door of opportunity wide open." Taryn was walking on the treadmill in her basement holding the phone to her ear while getting some exercise.

"Yes! Now you are getting it my dear." Socar was so proud of Taryn and how much she was maturing through the journey of discovering herself.

Taryn had decided it was time to deal with the pain of rejection. She was going to experience the hurt so that when the door to the fear of rejection finally closed, she would be able to walk through the open door of opportunity. This time she would appreciate and understand why the rejection was there, what it came to teach her and why it was necessary. If it was true that one man's loss was another man's gain, some awesome man would have a great treasure awaiting him whenever he found Taryn.

She wasn't giving up on her relationship with Aman, though. She was actually now viewing it through a completely different lens.

"I've been running from relationship to relationship for a while now and I've learned a lot. I now understand that no matter who I choose to be in a relationship with, I have to do the hard work of understanding that person, of loving that person the way he needs to be loved and most importantly of all, I have to love and understand myself first." Taryn gave Socar back her words to let her know that everything she had shared was finally sinking in.

"I've taught you well, daughter." They both shared a burst of laughter together as Socar lovingly teased Taryn.

Socar was beaming with pride that Taryn had finally come through the storm. She wasn't completely out of the woods yet, but she was well on her way.

"And let me remind you of this, Taryn, you will never be rejected by God. God's love for you is absolute, complete and unstoppable." Socar nearly sang this through the phone and it made Taryn do a little dance on the treadmill.

Taryn had learned so much about God's unconditional love for her in those days of learning to forgive herself and Aman. She knew that God's plan for her life was bigger than the mess she and Aman had made of their lives and of their relationship. God had given her so many revelations about herself through the journey. She was grateful to Socar for helping her sort through her feelings and emotions.

"Thank you so much. I could not have gotten through this difficult time without you. I thank God for you." Taryn slowed to do her cool down on the treadmill.

"Well, you're welcome! You've done some good work and I'm so proud of you, but you're not done yet. There's one more thing I need you to do. You know what you need to do?" Socar paused to give Taryn time to respond.

"I know! I know! Had I done this many years before, like you suggested when Ryan and I divorced, I probably wouldn't have made this new mess." Taryn sarcastically laughed. Socar had previously told her to get counseling. Now was prime time for her to get some professional help to deal with everything she had been through.

"Yep! You're right, once again, my dear. Do you still have the number I gave you?" Socar followed up with a chuckle.

"Yes ma'am! I have it and I will follow through this time." Taryn reassured Socar.

"I'll let her know you'll be coming." Socar was happy and relieved that Taryn was willing to get out of her comfort zone even more to find her way to complete healing.

"Thank you, once again, and I love you." Taryn ended the phone call.

She looked at her phone for a few moments before dialing Dr. Macey's office number. She scheduled an appointment with the receptionist for Monday of the following week.

CHAPTER 14

Ready to Give

"Give, and it will be given to you..." Luke 6:38 (NIV)

Upon arriving at Dr. Macey's office, Taryn was greeted by the receptionist who had her to complete all the intake forms. It was a quiet and peaceful setting tucked behind a fire station in an older three-story office building. Dr. Macey had made the entrance to her office space inviting, relaxing and a Zen place. After a short wait in the receptionist area, Taryn entered one of the counseling rooms where Dr. Macey was waiting for her sitting with a laptop on her lap. Once Taryn entered the counseling room, she noticed a short sofa facing two oversized bulky chairs. Taryn sat on the sofa across from Dr. Macey. The walls and all of the furniture were a neutral gray color that made the beautiful artwork and inspirational quotes hanging on the walls stand out.

"So, Taryn, what brings you to see me today?" Dr. Macey was a slender Caucasian woman who was about Taryn's height. She was in her mid-forties, yet her grey hair and conservative style of dress made her seem much older.

Taryn had been thinking a lot about how she would answer the "why are you here?" question. She knew Dr. Macey would ask, at least that's what she had seen depicted on television shows. When Dr. Macey asked Taryn why she had come to see her, Taryn lied. She lied because she was just too embarrassed about the whole situation with Aman. She felt stupid for being so naïve. It was easier for her to dance around the truth to try to avoid it. So, she just made up a story.

"This is about my son. I really want him to come see you. My son and I have been having some difficult interactions. His dad and I divorced a while ago, and it's been a challenging time for him ever since. His dad and I haven't been getting along lately either, and all of it is bothering me." Taryn looked Dr. Macey straight in the face and hid the truth because it hurt too much for her to hear herself say that truth. The painful truth was that she had been completely vulnerable and someone she loved and trusted had hurt her so deeply that it had shaken the very foundation of her belief in humanity.

Taryn wasn't ready to be that honest with a complete stranger. She carried on about Damon and Ryan for at least twenty minutes. Dr. Macey was highly skilled. From everything she heard Taryn say, it was evident Taryn's relationship with her son and her ex-husband wasn't the real reason she had come to see her. She questioned Taryn extensively about her relationship with Damon and Ryan. Taryn answered every question with a textbook answer which was a clear indication something important was missing. There was something more deeply disturbing to Taryn that she wasn't sharing. Dr. Macey frowned as if it didn't make sense to her that Taryn would come to see her now given that she and Ryan had been divorced for so many years. Also, other than their typical growing pains, Taryn hadn't described anything that seemed too abnormal about her relationship with her son, Damon, who was graduating and on his way to college and seemed to be doing quite well.

Dr. Macey was intrigued as she listened as Taryn kept things on a surface level with her. And then, somewhere along the conversation, Taryn finally felt comfortable opening up when Dr. Macey decided to pose another probing question.

"I noticed you've talked a lot about your son and your ex-husband, but how's your love life now?" Dr. Macey tilted her head slightly as she asked the question. Immediately Taryn's entire body shifted on the soft gray, houndstooth patterned couch, emphasizing Taryn's total discomfort with the question.

"Um, it's ok." Taryn shook her head slowly as she tried her best to respond authentically to the question.

Taryn rubbed her throat as a lump filled it. Her tear ducts overpowered her, and she couldn't hold it in anymore. Tears rolled down her face and she began to cry. Taryn shifted around on that couch as if she was going to burst open like a balloon that had been filled with too much hot air. She had to stop the façade so she could truly take advantage of the opportunity to tell Dr. Macey everything she had been going through in her relationship with Aman.

Dr. Macey pulled a few tissues from the box that was sitting on the table next to her. She handed them to Taryn as the tears continued rolling down her face like a faucet.

"Would you like some water?" Dr. Macey offered Taryn a moment to pause. Through Taryn's actions, Dr. Macey knew she was finally exposing the real reason Taryn was sitting on that couch in front of her.

Once Taryn got herself together, she shared everything that happened with Aman. She told Dr. Macey all about the start of their relationship. How she thought everything was going well and then one morning, by accident, she found out he had a four-year-old son and that he had been cheating on her for at least the first year of their relationship.

"I trusted him. Now that trust has been broken. I don't think I can be with him, but I am still deeply in love with him." Taryn grabbed two tissues to wipe her runny nose.

Taryn stumbled through all the emotional inner conflict that she felt each day, especially since he seemed so sincerely apologetic and acknowledged and owned how completely disturbing his behavior had been all those years. Once Taryn started talking, the floodgates opened, and she dumped it all. Dr. Macey listened carefully and took notes often on what Taryn shared. At the end when Taryn was finished, she offered her words of comfort in an authentic, empathetic and understanding way that made Taryn feel relieved that she had opened up and let it all go.

"I know it was extremely difficult for you to come here today, Taryn, and to share part of your life's journey with me, especially the part that has caused you so much pain. I am grateful that you have entrusted me with this information. I want you to know that many people struggle in their relationships. You aren't alone." Dr. Macey looked intensely and compassionately at Taryn, and a human connection began to form.

"Surprisingly, I feel so much better. It was really hard to share that part, but I'm so glad I did." Taryn mustered up a smile as she breathed in deeply and let out a big sigh, sniffling through the last of her tears.

"What do you want Taryn?" This question echoed from Dr. Macey's lips and when it reached Taryn's ears, it burned like a wildfire through the emptiness of her cluttered mind to the hollows of her broken heart.

After a pregnant pause that activated Taryn's tear ducts again, she held her head down looking at the floor as if it somehow held the answer. "I don't know what I want. I thought I knew, but I really don't know."

"Okay, I think I know what we need to work on together. If you are in agreement, let's start working through some of the things you've shared today. Is that okay?" Dr. Macey smiled to let Taryn know she was with her and there for her.

"Yes, I think that's a good plan." Taryn smiled back and reached across to shake Dr. Macey's hand as she prepared to leave.

"Before you go, I have these assignments I want you to work through. They will help you clarify some things, and they will provide me some more information as I continue to support you." Dr. Macey handed Taryn a small black binder with worksheets in it.

"Don't forget to think about the question. I will see you in two weeks." Dr. Macey reminded Taryn as she closed the door behind her. Taryn exited the counseling room to the lobby area with her head held high. She was proud of herself for taking that big step of speaking the truth to Dr. Macey.

For the first time in a long time, Taryn felt a bit lighter, even though she knew there was quite a bit of work ahead for her to do. She was excited to have something else to focus on besides Aman. Day after day for the full two weeks until it was time to go back to see Dr. Macey, Taryn looked in the mirror and asked herself the question. When she got up in the morning and when she laid down at night, she would ask herself the question. She posted it on the upper right edge of her bathroom mirror on a bright yellow sticky note.

"What do I want?" Taryn said aloud as she stared at herself in the mirror. "It's such a simple question. Why don't I have a good answer? All this time, I've been so focused on all this other stuff, all these other people and entirely missing what I want and need for me to be okay." Taryn drove in to work that next morning with the question still ringing in her spirit.

Dr. Macey had assured Taryn that she could help her find her way to the answer. Taryn was amazed that in such a short time, Dr. Macey had been able to determine where the disconnect lay in Taryn's life and offer her that question to ponder. Taryn was most perplexed that she had not ever taken the time to think about this question... until now. Even more, it rattled her very core that she didn't have an answer.

For the most part, Taryn had an answer for where she wanted to go with her career and what she wanted to accomplish financially. She knew what Ryan had wanted out of their marriage and she tried to fulfill it. She knew what Damon needed from her as his mother and she worked to give her everything to him. She knew what Aman wanted and she had bent over backward trying to be a good friend, a trustworthy companion and an amazing lover to him. But for this question, at this particular time in her life, she was totally clueless about what she wanted and needed. She realized in that moment that she hadn't focused on herself in an awfully long time.

Taryn had to admit to herself that she was lost. Somewhere along the way in life she had not really invested in her own personal well-being. Not the part that truly mattered. She was getting out of life what she was putting into it. The sad part was that Taryn wasn't investing very much in herself. Everything she did was for others. She didn't ever stop to think about what she wanted out of her life and for her relationships. She had spent so much of her life focused on other people and what they needed or wanted. It was time for her to be selfish and turn her attention inward to answer this important and critical question that would allow her to set limits and boundaries with the people she chose to have in her life.

Taryn completed the assignments that Dr. Macey had given her to help better answer the question. She wrote in her journal…

Dr. Macey gave me assignments to complete that push me to think about what I value. I had to think about this for a minute because I don't know if I have ever really taken the time to be explicit about what I value or what I want. I've been living life through my values, we all do. But this is the first time that I'm taking time to write them down. Seeing my values on paper is causing me to look at the decisions I've made over the years. I can now see where there is misalignment with what I value and what's important to me with some of the decisions that I've made for my life. It's hard to admit that I've been choosing things for me that don't align with what I truly value. I'm the only one responsible. I'm the only one who can change this. I will change it.

Taryn stared at the words on the page. She began praying for wisdom, insight and understanding of self as she continued to read through the materials Dr. Macey had shared that required her to write a life plan that aligned with her values as she lived out her heart's desire. It felt good to Taryn to be focusing on herself. The one thing she learned was she was the only person she could control. She was the only one who had complete and total control over her emotions, and she could manage and change them at any point that she decided to make changes. She felt empowered for the first time in way too long.

Ten weeks passed and Taryn had four additional counseling sessions with Dr. Macey. Taryn did the work she needed to do, and they produced major breakthroughs for her. In one of the assignments, Taryn had to face her fears. She sat across from Dr. Macey and they talked about her fears.

"I wouldn't have said that I was living in fear, but once I sat down and stopped to think about some of my actions, it was clear to me that I have been letting fear drive some of my actions." Taryn used hand gestures to explain herself to Dr. Macey.

"We all do. We're human, and some of the built-in defense mechanisms to protect us from hurt and disappointment can morph into fear. I'm glad you are breaking things down." Dr. Macey reaffirmed Taryn.

"I've learned that fear is something that can be unfounded, and most fears are birthed out of past trauma that is unresolved. I've been thinking a lot about my failed marriage. Some of the fears that I have around relationships have to do with not wanting to fail again or ever experience that kind of hurt again. I know I have to let go of those fears." Taryn shared her revelation with Dr. Macey.

In another session with Dr. Macey, Taryn examined how she resolved problems in her life through an assignment Dr. Macey gave her to complete.

"I know I have to first identify the root cause of the problem. I can think about possible solutions and understand that there are always blind spots in my thinking. I can ask others that I trust for their perspective, which can provide additional possible solutions. The point is to shift my thinking around the problem and to remain open to what I may be missing."

"Yes Taryn!" Taryn gave Dr. Macey a high five as Dr. Macey celebrated her growth in this area.

The third and fourth sessions with Dr. Macey were particularly important for Taryn in dealing with the situation with Aman. The assignments she completed for those sessions offered her the opportunity to build skills that would change her life for the better.

"Today, Taryn, we are going to talk about how to regulate your emotions. This is probably one of the most difficult things for any of my clients to learn to do. I want you to know that you will not leave here today with this exercise being a one-and-done. This will be ongoing work for you as it is for all of us. It really is the work that you will do forever." Dr. Macey smiled at Taryn.

"Okay, I'm ready." Taryn was open to the challenge and learning more about herself.

"You have to become more mindful of where in your body you feel your emotions when you are happy, sad, angry, afraid or excited. Pay attention to this more. Let's practice breathing. It can help you take control of your emotions." Dr. Macey led Taryn through some exercises.

After they finished the breathing exercises Dr. Macey asked, "How do you feel now?"

"More relaxed than when I came in. I feel like I can do this." Taryn nodded her head.

"Okay, I want you to practice it and we will talk about it in our next session. You've done great work! We're almost there, Taryn." Dr. Macey also gave Taryn another assignment for the next week.

"Before you go, one of the most important things we can do is set boundaries in our relationships with the people closest to us. I want you to think about what this means for you. What changes may need to happen so that you stay balanced...not giving too little or too much at any time." Dr. Macey sat back in the chair as Taryn left the office.

The next week Taryn came in with the completed assignments and the readings Dr. Macey gave her. They discussed Taryn's answers and examined Taryn's thinking and beliefs. At the end of it, Taryn learned that to receive what she wanted in her life, she had to be ready to give it away to herself first. She had to give herself love. She had to give herself truth. She had to give herself honesty. She had to be willing to examine and tear down some of the beliefs that she had subscribed to for far too long about herself. She had to focus on herself. It was hard work. It was so much easier to focus on Aman and everything he did. It was easier to look at his faults, imperfections and frailties and those of others she loved. It was so much harder to look within to see her faults, imperfections and frailties. Taryn acknowledged she was flawed, and she had to admit her struggles were just like Aman's and every other person on the planet. Once Taryn acknowledged this about herself, it was so much easier for her to understand others.

"To understand the human frailties of another person and to offer that person forgiveness instead of bitterness and anger is extremely powerful to renewing the human spirit. It would seem just the opposite. But God!" Taryn and Dr. Macey laughed in agreement as Taryn shared her final revelations with Dr. Macey.

They had become amazingly comfortable with one another over the weeks of meeting, and they both agreed their work together was just about complete.

"You've made tremendous progress and I'm so proud of you, Taryn." Dr. Macey commended Taryn on how well she had responded to counseling.

It was true. Taryn had grown so much over the weeks that they had been meeting.

"Thank you for helping me find myself again and for pushing me to the limit. I am forever grateful to you for it." Taryn promised Dr. Macey she would never lose focus of herself again.

Taryn realized losing herself wasn't worth it and it wasn't sustainable. She would never stop getting to know herself. She would never stop finding out what made her tick. Taryn had decided it would take forever for her to pursue her true authentic self, and it was a journey worth spending the rest of her lifetime pursuing.

"Yes! It takes forever to pursue you. Once you do that, you can be completely available to do the same with another person." Dr. Macey stood up and she and Taryn grabbed hands and held on for a while as Taryn prepared to leave her office for the final time.

"I want peace. I want joy. I want love and laughter in my life every day because that is the gift I give myself and others."

Taryn finally had the answer to Dr. Macey's question as she waved goodbye and disappeared out the counseling office door.

CHAPTER 15

Laugh at Life

"She's clothed in strength and dignity, and she laughs without fear of the future." Proverbs 31:25 (NLT)

Aman was waiting for Taryn to call. They were going on a date that evening. They planned to go out to dinner at one of their favorite restaurants and then to a comedy show. Taryn couldn't wait to share her final session with Dr. Macey with Aman. She and Aman had spent considerable time, over the weeks that she was in counseling, discussing the activities and processing everything new that Taryn was learning about herself.

Aman had also decided to go see a counselor. He was on a similar journey of self-discovery that helped him understand some of his toxic behavior choices. The counseling sessions gave him and Taryn a lot to think and talk about. It helped them clarify their true values while uncovering the areas where there was confusion and misalignment with their current behavior.

"I acknowledge the role that harmful beliefs and outdated thinking played in perpetuating negative behavior choices in our relationship." Taryn and Aman sat on the bar stools around the island in Taryn's kitchen. They talked before leaving for their evening out.

"I agree. I have held on to some of the nonsense for years and it it's finally time to let it go." Aman looked Taryn in the eye. He was serious about changing his behavior.

"I'm not responsible for your behavior, and your problems aren't mine to fix. As a friend, I can choose to support you, but ultimately the change is up to you." She pointed at Aman.

"You're right about that. I am determined to break free from the darkness that includes secrecy, hiding, lies and deceit so I can live a better life. I know that I have to live that life with or without you." He faced the reality and it was painful.

"From my final session with Dr. Macey, I now understand myself in the context of my relationship with you. I learned that my need to be a nurturer and caregiver is not necessarily a healthy role for me to play in your life or any man's life, for that matter. I have to set clear boundaries for myself and others. Every man is responsible for himself and fully capable of managing his own life. That includes my son and his father." Taryn snapped her finger in the air.

"Right on, Sister! I support and second that!" Aman smiled at Taryn as she stood up to get two wine glasses and poured them each a glass of red wine.

I feel so free." Taryn took a deep breath. "I don't have to try to control any part of our relationship. I can focus on myself and control me. It has given me a totally different perspective through which to view myself and our relationship." Taryn smiled her thousand-watt smile that Aman loved so much. She reached to sip her glass of red wine as she waited for Aman's response.

"Wow! That's really great that you had such breakthroughs in your sessions. You look refreshed, and I'm happy that you've healed in so many ways since seeing Dr. Macey." Aman smiled back at Taryn and then checked his watch. He pointed to it indicating it was time for them to leave for dinner.

"Boy, loving somebody sure is hard work. I guess that's why God made it a lifetime commitment, until death, huh?" Taryn grabbed her purse and held up her left hand to point to her ring finger as they headed toward the garage.

"Yep, it takes forever to figure it all out." He held up both his hands in surrender as they looked at each other and laughed out loud.

Taryn and Aman were working to rebuild the trust that had been broken in their relationship. Things were not perfect and sometimes it felt as if all hell could break loose if they left their egos unchecked, especially when something came up regarding Aman's son. Taryn had not fully reconciled that part of Aman's life and it would take some time for her to work through it. Yes, she and Aman loved each other. But in the words of the famous Tina Turner song, "What's love got to do with it?" Taryn knew it was going to take more than loving one another to have a strong, committed and lasting relationship. Her focus now was on building a friendship with Aman based on honesty, truth, integrity and loyalty. She knew they each had to do their individual work and in doing that work, it might take them down different paths. Taryn was learning to be okay with that, as hard as it was for them both.

That evening, Taryn and Aman sat across from one another at dinner and enjoyed honest, deep and stimulating conversation.

"I'm still struggling with you being the father of a young son. I don't know how to get past that." Taryn was honest with Aman.

"I understand that. Would it help if you met him? You want to see a picture of him?" He wanted her to know his son.

"Sure, I'd like to see a picture of him. I'm not so sure about meeting him." She shook her head.

Aman searched through his phone and showed her a picture of his son.

"Aw! He's a real cutie." Taryn smiled. He looked a lot like Aman.

"That's my boy. I'm amazed at him each time I see him. You would love him. I know you would." He beamed with pride.

"Probably so, but I don't believe a person should come in and out of kids' lives if that person doesn't plan to be there consistently. If we decide to continue our relationship in the future, maybe I can meet him, but not right now." Taryn shook her head back and forth.

"I understand. I don't think there's anything wrong with introducing my son to my friends and people I care about. Maybe one day." He was hopeful.

Taryn and Aman had learned to talk about the differences in their beliefs and values in a non-judgmental way. They questioned how they were raised and the values they learned to accept because of it.

"Who would you say was the most influential person in how you view intimate relationships today?" Aman posed that question to Taryn.

"Ummmm…I would have to think about that. I'd say I've had both negative and positive influences. Unfortunately, the negative ones are what I remember most. I would have to dig deep to think about positive ones. What about you? What would your answer be to that?" Taryn looked out the window of the restaurant at the view of the water surrounding them.

"It was definitely my uncle and aunt. I'm sure their relationship wasn't perfect, but they always look like they are happy. They always speak kindly to one another and I've never heard either of them say anything negative about one another to anyone in the family. They are definitely relationship goals." Aman ate a bite of his salad.

"Yeah, I would have to say my uncle and aunt too. They've been married for more than thirty years. I know it hasn't been all glory, but they have hung in there with each other. I love their commitment to sticking it out and making it work." Taryn buttered her bread.

"What do you think their secret to a successful relationship is?" he asked.

"I don't believe it's a secret. I believe it's hard work, and they do the hard work day-in-and-day-out, year after year. That's how you get anything done." Taryn was matter of fact.

"Agreed." Aman smiled at her.

"I also believe they let each other be. You know...they don't try to force each other to live up to their expectations. They love each other just the way they are. They leave room for each other to grow." Taryn revealed what she was hoping to have one day.

"I hear ya. I hope to get there one day." Their food arrived and they continued talking about what they believed about love and relationships and the impact of societal norms on gender roles for men and women in relationships.

Taryn affirmed that her self-value and worth as a woman didn't come from Aman or anyone outside of herself. Once Taryn shifted her perspective, she was no longer powerless over her emotions for Aman. She felt empowered to define the relationship in the context of her own standards and values and what she presently needed from the relationship. She no longer felt consumed with trying to build her life around making a relationship with Aman work, but instead she was truly free to build her life and allow the relationship to serve as an enhancement.

After dinner, they headed to a comedy show. Taryn and Aman laughed so hard until they cried at the comedy show. It was a great evening and Taryn appreciated their time together now more than ever. Between her challenges with Ryan, Aman, and her sometimes up and down relationship with Damon, Taryn almost got tripped up. But she didn't fall for it. She fought to reclaim the life she knew God desired for her. She was now stronger than she had ever been. She was more determined than ever to laugh every time life tried to break her. She was wiser now that she had walked through the challenges she had faced. Her faith had been tested and she had come out on the winning side. Not because everything was perfect, but because her thoughts about everything were different.

The night ended with Taryn and Aman sitting in front of her house reminiscing about the night and replaying the jokes the comedians told. Neither of them wanted the evening to end there.

"What do you need right now?" Taryn wasn't expecting an answer from Aman, but she wanted to reassure him that he had the answers.

"I'm still learning what I need." Aman thoughtfully paused before answering Taryn's question. She accepted his answer because it was his truth. They decided it was best that Aman leave. He kissed her on the cheek, and they ended the evening.

Taryn was grateful for everything the experiences with Aman had taught her about trusting God. By the grace of God, she had passed the tests and there were no limits to what God could do. She was healed, happy, healthy and strong and she owed it all to God.

Before going to bed that night, Taryn looked out her window and up into the sky. "I can't wait to wake up tomorrow. I'm looking forward to Sunday morning worship at church." When she got to church that Sunday, she made her way to the altar and kneeled down to pray.

"Father God, thank you so much for forgiving me, for loving me, for washing me and making me clean. Father, I trust You with my life. I give myself to You. I live for You. I honor You. You are worthy, Father God. Thank You! Thank You! Thank You!" Taryn burst into an audible praise at the altar of the church because she had survived some of the toughest moments of her life and she had learned to find peace and strength through it all.

After church, Taryn and Socar met for brunch. Socar wanted to catch up and hear all about the new adventures in Taryn's life.

"People can change. I've changed through this whole process." Taryn looked Socar in the eye as she poured maple syrup all over her already-buttered pancakes.

"You're right, honey. People can change. I can definitely see a huge change in you. I'm so proud of you for putting your big girl panties on." Socar and Taryn laughed so hard as they thought back over the months before when Taryn was a total and complete mess.

"You know, I couldn't have imagined that I would be here. I was so broken a few months ago. It took me fully understanding me, not through the lens of a man, but through God's eyes. Through Him, with help from you and Dr. Macey, I was able to become healed, whole, and complete. Look at what God has done." Taryn raised both hands in the air in praise to God.

"Hallelujah! He is a good God." Socar followed Taryn's lead and also raised her hands in the air.

The two of them spent hours in the restaurant talking and making plans for their next outing. They were planning a spa date where they would each get a massage, a manicure and pedicure. It was late afternoon and the brunch had ended. They decided it was time to leave. They stood up at the table and headed toward the exit. Once they were in the parking lot, Socar had one last piece of advice for Taryn.

"Taryn, as you move forward, please make sure you use wisdom as you listen and obey God." Socar grabbed Taryn's hand and held it to ensure she heeded her words.

"He has a specific direction and big plans for your life, baby girl. Remember to not take yourself so seriously…laugh at yourself because sometimes you can be completely stubborn and bull headed. You know I will always tell you the truth." Socar pulling Taryn close, gave her a hug.

"I know. I know." Taryn chuckled as she rested her head on Socar's shoulder.

"I've been headstrong since I was a little girl. Everyone told me that as a kid." Taryn kissed Socar on the cheek. They said their goodbyes and got in their cars.

Taryn acknowledged that quality made her a natural leader. However, there was still more work for her to do. She had to follow God's plan for her life and watch it unfold. She didn't want to get ahead of Him. She also knew she had a responsibility to share her experiences with others. Her story wasn't as pretty on the inside as her life may have seemed to some on the outside. The inside view included multiple failures and several disappointments as it related to relationships, losing herself, and not taking time to understand the plan God had for her life. She needed to share it with others as part of the healing process because somebody somewhere needed to know how she turned her lemons into lemonade. If she could help one woman, one man, one young person or even future generations avoid the painful heartbreak and sheer turmoil that her ignorance had caused in some of her most important relationships, it was all completely worth it.

Taryn was going to take Socar's advice and laugh more. She knew laughter was medicine for the soul. Life had a way of giving Taryn many things to laugh about. In spite of it all, at the end of the day she was a winner. When she lay down to sleep that night, she prayed.

"Father, I thank you because you have kept me another day. I know I can help someone else navigate through this life. Please show me how I can help someone else and I won't ever stop."

Taryn fell asleep laughing. God has a sense of humor.

CHAPTER 16

Don't Ever Stop

"Let us not become weary in doing good, for at the proper time we will reap a harvest if we do not give up." Galatians 6:9 (NIV)

"How deep are you willing to go?" Taryn smiled like a young child opening presents on Christmas morning. She looked Aman right in the eye as she leaned across the island steadying both elbows on the granite countertop, resting her chin on her fists.

She woke up that Sunday morning with a bright idea that the two of them should write a book together. It seemed unbelievable that God would drop something like that into her spirit. She immediately called Aman and insisted that he be at her house by ten o'clock. She wanted him to answer the question without trying to find the nearest exit. She changed the subject for a minute to distract him from becoming more anxious about what she asked him. Taryn knew this might be too much for Aman, yet she wasn't going to give him an opportunity to run this time. Aman had a frightened look all over his face and from past experience he could completely shut down without giving her idea any consideration.

"It's okay. We can do this Aman. We have to do this." Taryn walked over to Aman, touching him on the shoulder to reassure him that he could share his concerns about what she was asking. She wouldn't judge him even though she'd be disappointed if he totally refused the idea God had given her.

"I don't want to do this right now, Taryn. Why do you need to do this?" Aman stepped back from Taryn with a confused look on his face. He had been blindsided by her request. He pushed back on her idea even though he never liked to argue with Taryn.

"Because…it's important to me. That's why we have to do it. Because it could help us. It could help others." Taryn pointed her finger back and forth at Aman and herself. She wondered if it was a good idea, after all, since things had changed so drastically between the two of them. Maybe it didn't matter anymore.

"I'm not sure what good digging up the past is going to do. We've already moved past all this." Aman pleaded with Taryn to leave well enough alone.

"Look, I know it's risky, Aman. But in order for us to truly move forward, we have to dig up the root of these problems. We have to expose them. We have to be completely vulnerable with one another and with others. Otherwise, we may continue to stumble. Then, all of this was for nothing." Taryn looked out her living room window as if she could see the future.

The two of them had calmed down and were speaking in a softer tone to one another. They had moved from the kitchen to the window seat in her living room. Taryn and Aman faced each other.

"We can't ever stop questioning ourselves. We can't get comfortable where we are. We have to keep moving forward and sometimes that means doing the difficult work of rewriting our own story. Our story could help those who aren't married understand what they need to know before entering marriage. It could give them some things to think about and examine to see if they are really ready for marriage. Could they love and forgive someone when things are far from perfect, whey they've been hurt and their lives shattered?" Taryn was giving Aman her best sales pitch to convince him to take what would be an incredible life changing journey with her.

"I don't know about this, Taryn." They spent a few hours talking about Taryn's idea of writing a book together.

"Let's weigh the pros and cons of this." Taryn took out a piece of paper and divided it down the middle of the page and wrote "Pros" and "Cons" at the top of each half of the page.

"Okay…one con is what people will think." Aman pointed to the con side of the page and Taryn wrote it down.

"Yes, of course! We both have to think about how others in our lives might be affected by this. There will be an impact." Taryn acknowledged Aman's concern.

"I've hurt enough people in my life and I have to think about how anything I do moving forward might affect others, especially my son." Aman looked Taryn in the eye.

"On the other hand, it's a chance to leave a roadmap to our children and grandchildren of what not to do. We could change the game. Break some generational curses." Taryn wrote that on the Pros side of the page.

"You're right! Let me think about it for a while." At least now, Aman was willing to give more thought and consideration to what Taryn was proposing.

"Ok, that's fair. I respect that you need more time to process it all. Just don't take too much time." Taryn threw up her hands in response to Aman's apprehension.

They both laughed and shifted the conversation to their plans for the day. Aman left, but he was coming back later after running some errands so they could talk more about her idea. Taryn sat for a few hours in her window seat outlining the book and journaling her ideas as they came to her.

I had a dream the night before that Aman and I had written a book. I saw us standing before a large crowd of men and women talking about our personal relationship journey. In my dream, I saw Aman sharing his story with the men. After he finished talking, I saw myself speaking with the women. We were traveling around the world sharing our story and helping couples heal. The dream seemed so real, and I believe it is a next step for us. As weird as it seems neither of us have ever written a book before, but I believe we can do it. I hope he's willing to at least give it a try.

Taryn didn't just want to take the valuable lessons she had learned with her to the grave, she wanted to use them to help others, especially her future grandchildren. With all that she endured with Ryan and her experiences with Aman, she would never be the same. She was wiser. She was stronger. She was even more grateful for every lesson those relationships had taught her as she looked back on it all. She was sure that she needed to help other women and men navigate the difficulties of relationships to make everything that she had gone through worth it.

It was perfect for Taryn to do this book with Aman because he had done his own work. He had realized how lost he was, and he had humbled himself so he could learn to make better decisions. If he agreed to do this with her his entire life would be more enriched because of it. Now that Aman was more open to sharing, he could influence other men. In their private conversations, Aman often shared how so many of the men in his circle needed information and opportunities to talk about their lives without judgment.

"So many men need opportunities to heal from broken-ness, disappointment, failure and bad decisions." Aman held his head up this time when he spoke. In the past, the shame would cause him to look down or look away from Taryn.

"So many men need to hear your story." Taryn would tell Aman every time they talked about their journey together. He had finally accepted her forgiveness and if more men would break their silence with one another it would help them avoid being so careless in destroying their own lives and the lives of the people they love.

It was also time for Taryn to stop living in the past. She had to give herself the gift of forgiveness as she looked forward to a bright future. Something amazing was waiting for her there. The sooner she left the past behind, the sooner she could get to all the future held for her. On occasion, she would get a glimpse of what a life could look like in a healthy, supportive and loving relationship. For now, Taryn was learning not to focus too much on the future and miss the opportunity to enjoy the present moments with the people who meant the most to her. She would leave the future in God's capable hands. He was well able to handle his business where all areas regarding her future were concerned.

Grandma Bella would have been proud of the woman Taryn had become. Taryn admitted she had come a long way and there was still so much more work for her to do in her own life. This new idea was going to set her up for helping people. It was something she always wanted to do. At this point, she needed her life to be about more than just her wants, needs and desires being met. She wanted to do something with her life that would give her great joy and fulfillment. She prayed and asked God for wisdom to truly live out her life's purpose. This new idea that came to her in her dream seemed to fit the puzzle perfectly. In her quiet time of reflection, God reminded Taryn that He had accelerated all of her goals that she had set for herself. God was speaking to her that it was now time for her to do His work.

"God, you said you've accelerated my plans and now it's time for me to do Your work. What does that mean?" This scared her and exhilarated her at the same time.

Taryn was at a point in her life where the future outweighed her fears and she was determined to find out. She couldn't waste any more of her precious time on meaningless work or relationships because relationships mattered most to her.

"It's the people in your life that make it rich and amazing." Zoah often spoke those words to her family. Taryn now spoke them to herself.

It didn't matter if Taryn lived more than a thousand miles away from family; they were always a priority in her life. She thought of her son, Damon, and how he was growing into a fine young man who would one day have his own children. She was so proud of him. Their relationship had changed over the last year, partly because she let go and Damon asserted himself and demanded his independence as he spread his wings in the world.

Taryn was grateful for the amazing friends she had in her life. Her true friends were few, and if she had one true friend, she was a wealthy woman. She was a wealthy woman indeed because she had more than one. She thought of Socar and how she had loved and mentored her through some of the most difficult times in her life. She was grateful for her friendship and mentorship.

"Taryn don't waste your time on things and people that do not align with your core values and your life's work. If he, she, or it does not bring you to your higher self, it has to go, no matter how difficult it is for you to let it go." Socar's words impacted Taryn as if she was sitting right there in that moment speaking them, but Taryn was sitting alone quietly in her window seat looking out at the sun reflecting off the fountain in her yard.

"Sometimes this is easier said than done. When my heart is involved, it's hard. But I know it's necessary." Taryn wrote the words in her journal based on her last phone conversation with Socar where she agreed with the wisdom she was sharing. She was learning to accept the truth of Socar's words because she wanted to go where God was taking her. It wasn't going to be a road everyone could travel.

She sat in the quiet of her living room and the sun began to set. "I wonder if Aman will be part of the next phase of my journey or if he will decide to exit my life." She had invited him to come along by sharing the book idea with him. She was willing to give him time to think about it because it would be a big step for him. She wasn't sure if he would decide to walk alongside her or not. Taryn was going to be okay either way.

"It's bigger than me and Aman. I have to do this with or without him." Taryn understood the desire in her heart was bigger than the shame and guilt that both of them had felt in the past months as they dealt with everything. Taryn desired to be married again. Aman desired it too. Day-by-day, they were both dealing with the scars left on their souls. Taryn was hopeful that one day they would get past it and give marriage another try even if it was with other people.

"Only God knows whether it is for me to marry Aman." Taryn reasoned that she would not dwell on it and that in God's perfect timing she would know who her next husband would be.

Taryn was so much more equipped this time around to handle the responsibility of marriage. She understood the seriousness of the work that marriage required and the reward that came with putting in the work and enjoying the return on that investment. Taryn desired to get marriage right the next time. If she did marry Aman, he would definitely be the man to keep her on her knees in prayer.

"Father God, if Aman isn't the man for me, please send me the man that I can partner with and share the rest of my life with. Lord help us to fulfill Your purpose and Your promise for our life together." Taryn prayed this prayer in faith, and she trusted God to bring it to pass.

Taryn had watched God restore her friendship with Aman even though it looked impossible at one point. It made Aman so upset when Taryn wanted to end their relationship, and they were both ready to walk away multiple times. But God! All the time, it was the perfect recipe for God to deliver on His promises. Sometimes relationships had to die in order for God to resurrect something new and amazing. She was not worried about her future husband. God would do it. She was walking by faith and not by sight.

"God, I'm going to be like Peter who stepped out of that boat and locked in on Jesus allowing him to walk on that water. I'm not taking my eyes off You." Taryn had to keep her focus on God and His unlimited potential to bring exactly who she needed into her life. It was just a matter of time.

Life's events proved to Taryn that God used imperfect people and imperfect situations in the Bible to change lives. She witnessed God, in His sovereign wisdom, take dreadful situations in her own life and turn them around and use them for her good just as the word promised. Taryn was thankful that she witnessed God move in her life and she was certain that His promises for her life would come to pass. As she sat there pondering all God had done and writing about it in her journal, the doorbell rang. It was Aman.

"Hey, how are you? You all finished running your errands?" Taryn allowed Aman space to step inside. She greeted him with a hug.

"Yep! I've thought a lot about your idea. Boy, there is never a dull moment with you, Taryn." Aman smiled that smile that made Taryn fall in love with him in the first place.

"So, do you have an answer for me?" Taryn anxiously awaited Aman's response. She stopped mid-step to turn and look at him to see if she could read which direction he was going in with his response.

"Hold on, hold on. First, we need to talk about a few things." Aman seemed open to the idea.

She invited him into the kitchen to have a seat. Aman asked really good questions. He wanted to know if the book would be about communication.

"You know, Taryn, so much of what I've learned is that we as men, we don't really know how to communicate. We don't communicate as well with one another as women do in relationships. We need help with that." It was clear Aman had really taken time to think more deeply about her idea and it made Taryn beam with pride.

"Yes, communication is key." Taryn didn't want to interrupt him, but she wanted to let him know she was listening to every word he was saying. She was proud of him for sharing his heart.

"We also have to talk about love. Not just love like, I love you, but love like what it means to genuinely love someone. You know the kind of love that forgives. You know like the love in Corinthians. That's what men need because we are definitely going to mess up." Taryn and Aman laughed out loud as they both said the word Corinthians in unison and shook their heads back and forth.

"Yes, Aman, once you love someone, I mean truly love someone, you never stop loving them. The energy may transfer, but it's still always there." Taryn added her two cents to what Aman was saying.

"You know men, we dream big. We need a woman who will support our dreams, even when they seem silly and crazy. Especially, when they are silly and crazy." Aman pointed his finger at Taryn to make his point.

"Um hm. Yep, what we say we can have, we can have it. What we dream, we can have. We can have it all when we support one another." Taryn was agreeing with everything Aman was saying and it seemed like his answer was going to be yes.

"Ok, so that's it, we have to love one another and forgive one another. We have to learn from our mistakes and show compassion. We have to walk with one another with understanding that there is no lack in the Earth, only abundance. There is power in love. When we connect, we have to believe that. Where love is involved, we have to find a way even if we have to make a way or create a way. There's always a way. And finally, we have to love ourselves." Aman stood up and walked around the kitchen.

He wasn't talking to Taryn anymore; he was talking to himself. The idea was beginning to resonate with him, and he was owning it and creating an outline. Taryn started recording what he was saying in her journal. After Aman finished, Taryn knew this story needed to be told.

"God, please let him say yes. God can we do this?" Taryn prayed softly under her breath and she asked God for permission to tell their story. The response she heard echo in her spirit was, "Move forward, I got this."

They had to do it. It wouldn't be easy. It could make everything even more complicated. But it could also make them even more open to living life without fear.

"Will you write this book with me? Will you take this incredible life changing journey with me?" Taryn's heart was pounding in her chest as she stood in front of Aman holding both his hands, awaiting his response. She was still silently praying he would say yes.

Aman squeezed Taryn's hands tighter. He looked down at the floor for a long time to gather his thoughts. He took in a deep breath and sighed deeply as he let it out.

"I…" Just as Aman began to speak, Taryn's phone rang.

The phone was sitting on the island in the kitchen next to where they were standing. They both looked down at the phone at the same time. The screen read "Unknown Caller."

"I'll ignore that." Taryn turned her attention back to Aman.

"Are you sure? You can get it." Aman encouraged Taryn to answer it because it would give him more time to think about what he was about to say.

Taryn picked up the phone, as it rang again, annoyed that she and Aman were being interrupted.

"Okay! Excuse me. Hello!" Taryn expected it to be a sales call.

"This is a collect call from a correctional facility. Will you accept the call?" The recording said.

"Oh my God! Yes, I will accept." Taryn's eyes bulged as she prepared for the worst news she had heard all day.

"Taryn, it's Ryan." The voice said.

"Ryan?" Taryn looked at Aman.

"Please don't hang up." Ryan sounded weak. "I'm in trouble and I need your help."

Taryn shook her head in disbelief. Why would Ryan be calling her, of all people, asking for help? She sat down quickly with her head in her hands as she listened to him speak. Her excitement for Aman's answer was now totally deflated as she listened to Ryan and became consumed with nausea as he spoke…

Epilogue

Birthing Me

I am giving birth to life that will help others through life.

As a woman, I am birthing everything around me.

I am birthing new openness to expanding my mind and my heart.

Birthing requires me to confront fears within myself.

It requires me to question that which I've based my foundation of beliefs and values on.

I am uprooting the fears.

I am questioning the fears and the purpose they have served in my life.

Do they serve the purpose today?

What am I learning now about myself?

I can't lose.

I am a winner because I stay open to learning more about myself and others.

I am birthing something new in my life.

I am happy to be in this space.

I am birthing my next open door.

I am birthing love and light into my life.

I am this brilliant love of God.

I am compassionate with all that God is birthing through me right now.

I acknowledge the birthing process can be painful sometimes.

And the pain is necessary to bring forth the newness of life.

I am nurturing the pain.

It has something to teach me about love.

I am birthing my mind which holds the key to healing every part of my being.

I am birthing love and light from my mind.

I am birthing the best part of me.

I am birthing the best of everything for me, my family and my friends.

I am birthing openly for all to see.

I am birthing connectedness and love.

I am birthing insight and wisdom of the universe and all it has to offer me.

I am love.

I am light.

I am birthing me.

Until Love

CHAPTER 1

Reunited

Greater love has no one than this, that he lay down his life for his friends. John 15:13 (BSB)

Taryn was surprised when Ryan announced her phone number was the only one he knew by heart when he got his one phone call from jail. She cringed because Aman was listening the whole time as Ryan spoke to her like she was still his wife. Aman could hear him clearly through her cell phone and he was staring Taryn down the whole time. She tried to adjust the volume on her phone without Aman seeing, but she couldn't hear Ryan.

"I don't have a lot of time. Do you have something to write with?" Ryan was whispering yet his tone was demanding.

"Yes, go ahead." Taryn turned away from Aman and held the phone with her shoulder as she wrote what Ryan said.

"I'm in Cleveland, Ohio at the county lock up and the number is…"

"Ryan, what are you doing in Cleveland, Ohio?" Taryn interrupted him and looked back at Aman.

"I promise I will tell you everything, please just write this down and see if you or someone can come and get me. Please, Taryn."

"Okay, okay! Go ahead."

"I have a review hearing in the morning. It's likely they will let me out, but someone will need to post bond. Right now, my bond is two thousand dollars. You will need ten percent of that so it will be two hundred dollars."

Taryn wrote down all the information he gave her and repeated it back to him to make sure she had it correct.

"Yes, that's it. Thank you. Please see if you can post bond. Maybe you can do it for me over the phone."

"Ryan, I have no idea how to do any of this. I don't even know where to start with this. What happened?"

"Taryn I gotta go!" He rushed his words. "I'll see if they will let me call tomorrow, but please see what you can do."

"Okay Ryan. I'm praying for you. God is with you no matter where you are." Taryn reminded him.

Taryn ended the call. She was speechless. Aman was in disbelief too. He knew they had a troubled past and he was just as surprised for Taryn to get that call.

Taryn was silent as she sat in shock and disbelief.

"What was that all about?" Aman broke the silence with a confused look on his face as he pointed to the phone.

"I have no idea." Taryn was staring off in the distance shaking her head back and forth slowly.

"So much for our conversation." Aman threw up his hands.

"I'm pissed that Ryan expects me to help him as if I have no choice. He spouted off information to me just as he did when we were married. Stupid me didn't refuse to write it down or just hang up on him. I could only think of Damon."

"I understand." Aman came up from behind her to give her a bear hug.

"I've got to tell Damon. Oh Lord! How am I going to tell him? He's going to be devastated." Without understanding the depths of Ryan's issues, Taryn put her hand over her mouth as she immediately started praying under her breath for her son. Whatever Ryan was into, him being in jail, would hurt Damon. He adored his father. But Taryn knew what she had to do. Calling Damon would tear her up, but he was old enough to know what was going on, and Taryn needed to know, too.

She dialed her son's number, but before the call could connect, she whispered to God, "Lord, please help me..."

CPSIA information can be obtained
at www.ICGtesting.com
Printed in the USA
FSHW012126220420
69262FS

9 781733 486484